The Adventures of Jasmine Turmalina

ii

The Adventures of Jasmine Turmalina

Henry Stark

With

Illustrations by Florence Lavan

and

Rhymes contributed by Barry Bernstein

iv

For Jessica Stark

The real Jasmine Turmalina.

A Warning to Children

This book serves as a warning to those children who disobey their parents and venture into their backyards when everyone else has gone to sleep.

There are many strange things that go on in the backyard when the sun goes down. Mysterious creatures, with heads made of wax, playing haunting melodies, appear out of nowhere to kidnap dolls. Crafty, two-dimensional, Tilops emerge from woodsheds to steal all your belongings. And—worst of all—the Craxies will...Oh! It is best not to talk about the Craxies!

Children: heed your parents' warnings! Even if you escape from these creatures of the night, you will not be able to resist the call from the hollow maple tree in the back of the yard where you have always feared to go, even in daylight. And once you enter the hollow of the maple tree there is no turning back.

Because in the hollow of the maple tree, there is a tunnel that leads to a place from which there is no escape. And to enter this place you must pass a door that says:

*Lasciate ogne speranza, voi ch'intrate**

"Give up all hope ye who enter here"

*With apologies to Dante Alighieri in the "Inferno".

viii

Adventures of Jasmine Turmalina

1. Jasmine goes into the garden

One Sunday morning in the middle of April, Jasmine felt restless and moody. She didn't like it when her mother told her to clean up her room and she liked it even less when her father told her to wash her face and brush her teeth. Even her favorite doll Sochi who slept in Jasmine's bed seemed unhappy with her. Sochi didn't sleep well because Jasmine kicked too much in bed and kept waking Sochi up. But being only a doll what could Sochi say? I mean Sochi lived in Jasmine's house, ate Jasmine's food, played with Jasmine's toys, and had a warm bed to sleep in at night. So where would Sochi go? Who would take her in if she left the Jasmine household? Anyway being only a doll Sochi couldn't walk very far on her own and depended on Jasmine to take her to her favorite places like the dollhouse museum, the dollhouse zoo, and, best of all, the dollhouse park where she could meet other dolls including the handsome superdoll Jacksnap

Jasmine walked out of the kitchen door and into the backyard carrying Sochi. The leaves on the trees—while still small— were a bright light green, some of the flowers had already come up, the robins were feasting on worms and the scrapulas were plocking away. Jasmine even saw a caterpillar talking to a scrapula but when she leaned over to hear what they were saying, they stopped talking and looked annoyed. "How would you like it if we listened in on your conversation," said the caterpillar, whose name was Optimus. "I wouldn't care," said Jasmine. "And anyway you couldn't be talking about anything important. What do caterpillars know? They have small brains and can only talk foolish gossip like which caterpillar is ready to turn into a butterfly and what are the latest styles for butterfly wings and other such nonsense."

Upon hearing these harsh words Hypolux the scrapula began to plock loudly and Optimus the caterpillar got angry. "First of all I do not have a small brain in relation to the size of my body. My brain weighs a tenth of an ounce but my body only weighs one ounce. So my brain is one tenth as big as my body. But your brain, Jasmine, weighs one pound and you weight 70 pounds so that your brain is only one seventieth the size of your body. So ounce for ounce I am much smarter than you. Second of all we *are* talking about important things. My friend Hypolux here was telling me that some of the scrapulas, who can't sleep at night, heard strange night sounds coming out of the hollow of that big maple tree in the corner of the yard. If you don't think it's important to know what's making those sounds, then *you* are being foolish! Why there might be evil creatures living there that might kidnap us or worse!"

Jasmine laughed. "Strange sounds my foot! What you are hearing is the wind shaking the branches and the buds exploding into leaves. But if you like I'll investigate these 'strange night sounds' that the scrapulas are hearing. Tonight, after it gets dark, Sochi and I will go to the maple and see what is going on. I will report to you in the morning about what we found out!"

Hypolux, Optimus, Jasmine, and Sochi

When Sochi heard that Jasmine was going to inspect the hollow maple tree at night, she froze with fear. Every smart doll knows that the night belongs to all kinds of scary creatures that you never see during the day. Why Sochi had heard of a dollnapper by the name of Waxface who had dollnapped at least thirty dolls and sold them to pirates who roamed the Arabian Sea! Whatever became of those dolls no one ever found out but there were plenty of rumors. One rumor was that the stuffing was taken out of the dolls and used to make pillows, which were then sold to Eskimos. Another rumor was that the dolls were sold to an evil circus owner who gave them away as prizes in the tents where people played games. And the worst rumor of all was that the dolls were sold to people who covered then in porcelain and sold them as 'original art' to rich people who lived in New York City on Park Avenue.

Waxface did his dollnapping at night. He played this haunting tune on his flute, which only young girls, dolls and scrapulas could hear. But scrapulas are very intelligent and cannot easily be fooled. When one young, inexperienced, scrapula left his nest to see who was playing this wonderful tune, the adult scrapulas would begin to plock like crazy and the young scrapula was dragged back to his nest. But with the dolls it was a different story. Often the dolls were put away into closets for the night where they were lonely and cold. Even dolls that were not put into closets but lived on desks, tables, and what have you often felt neglected at night. Oh, if they could only join their owners in a warm comfortable bed! But many people and even some children had no regards for the feelings of dolls. These were the dolls who were most likely to be dollnapped by Waxface. The dolls found the tune irresistible and followed the melody no matter where it led. When these dolls heard his haunting tune, they began to imagine a better life. A life where people paid attention to them, loved them, took them on trips, treated them kindly, and even gave them Italian ice-cream. So when they heard Waxface's music they went to him. And that was the last anyone ever saw or heard from them!

It wasn't just dollnappers that Sochi feared. It was well-known that Tilops came out a night and they would sometimes steal your clothes, your money, your ribbons and gold stars, and even your socks. Tilops didn't only steal from dolls but even from humans of all ages. Here is how Tilops operated. They would approach their victim and say something like: "If you give me your hat, I'll tell you where you can find a genie who will grant you a wish," Then the victim, who very often would be a young boy or girl who had no business being out at night anyway, would hand over his or her hat and the Tilop would write the address of the genie on a piece of paper, for example

Mr. Rex Geenie

3510 Decatur Avenue,

Bronx, NY 10113

Then the victim would write Mr. Rex Geenie asking for a pony or a pet alligator. But Mr. Geenie was not a real genie in the sense of someone who could magically grant wishes. Mr. Geenie was a mailman and the only "wish" that he could grant was to deliver the mail. So naturally the victim was disappointed. No pony, no pet alligator, and no HAT!

But of all the creatures that came out at night it was the Craxies that Sochi feared the most. The Craxies would come out only in the dead of night and looked really scary. The head of a Craxie looked like the head of a rabbit but the rest of him looked like the bottom half of a frog. But it wasn't the appearance of the Craxie that frightened Sochi so much. The really scary thing about the Craxies was the tricks they pulled on dolls and children who were out in the middle of the night. One of their favorite tricks was to put glue on rocks, trees, lawns and other places that children or dolls might touch. Once the child or doll was smeared by the glue it couldn't get away and the Craxies would come out with little buckets of smelly paint and paint the child or doll with weird colors like blue and purple or pink and green. The glue didn't stick too long, maybe only two or three hours but while it stuck all of the night creatures such as rabbits, foxes, owls, bats, moles, and walking fish would come out and laugh their heads off while looking at the little girl victim painted green with pink hair and her yellow and lavender painted doll.

If the shame of being painted by the Craxies wasn't bad enough, imagine having to face your parents in the morning with a weirdly painted face and having to explain how it happened. Of course there had to be some sort of punishment like not being allowed to have desert for a whole week or not being allowed to sleep-over at your best friend's house for a month. Sometimes when the little girl was being extra difficult and still went out at night, to risk being painted by the Craxies, or swindled by the Tilops, or having her doll kidnapped by Waxface, the parents became really angry and decided to send the girl to the Better Behavior Academy for Non-Obedient Girls known as BEBE for short. BEBE was run and guarded by very stern women dwarfs who did not tolerate any nonsense. These dwarfs were called Monitors and, in keeping with being short, had short names like Sister Ta or Sister Ba or Sister Ca or Sister Ze. To keep order they walked around with tickle sticks. If you were touched by a tickle stick you laughed until your sides hurt. BEBE was located in an old castle with creaky stairs and a large, cold, attic where the dwarfs kept spider farms. The spider webs were used for making silk shoes for the Monitors who had very sensitive and delicate feet. The castle had all kinds of mysterious rooms, many of which were locked during the day and unlocked only at night. If you were sent to BEBE you could take only one doll with you and with Sochi's luck it would surely be Sochi that Jasmine would take with her if Jasmine were sent there. Life at BEBE was no picnic. First of all, all the little girls staying at BEBE had to get up at five in the morning and be ready to collect spider webs by six in the morning. You may well ask why six in the morning? At that time the spiders were sleepy from weaving their webs the day before and could not prevent the harvesting of their webs. Second of all the food wasn't very good. At breakfast the little girls were given a potato sandwich which consisted of a sliced cooked potato between two slices of organic bread, and a glass of milk. For lunch there was a glass of pear juice and a bowl of oxtail soup. Dinner was the worst: tomato puree with white kidney beans and calf's foot jelly for desert. All this was very nutritious of course but not the kind of food that little girls like to eat.

These thoughts made Sochi cringe with fear. Why couldn't Jasmine be like the other little girls in the neighborhood who were well-behaved and much less adventurous?

Jasmine and Sochi

2. Jasmine has diner with her family

At exactly 6:30 PM, Jasmine's mother Chacha called her to have dinner. Jasmine's father Caesar was already sitting at the table reading the newspaper. Jasmine was unhappy because that afternoon her friend Dorvit had told her that she, Jasmine, was only her *second* best friend and that Pilata, the girl across the street, was Dorvit's *first* best friend. Jasmine had wanted to be Dorvit's *first* best friend. So, in response, Jasmine had told Dorvit that she, Dorvit, was Jasmine's *second* best friend and that Sochi was Jasmine's *first* best friend. "Ha-ha!" Dorvit had said, "So you admit that only a doll could be your *first* best friend. That shows that I am more popular than you since my first best friend is a human!" Jasmine had forgotten that

Sochi was only a doll and therefore had no reply to Dorvit's taunt. This irritated Jasmine but she didn't want to become Dorvit's *third* best friend by saying something that might make Dorvit angry. So she kept quiet and merely said *see you later* and then walked away.

When she sat down at the table to eat, Caesar asked her if she had washed her hands. "Yes, Daddy," she replied, I washed my hands." "With soap?" Caesar asked. "No, Daddy, just with water. I figured that the water would drown all the little germs on my hands left over from playing with snails and caterpillars out in the garden. I know that germs can't swim so they must have drowned when I rinsed my hands." Caesar looked at her for several seconds, shook his head and said, "No, darling that's not how it works. The little germs get washed off by using soap and water. The soap makes your hands slippery and the water rinses them off. Also soap contains chemicals that are not healthy for germs so that many of them get killed when you wash your hands. Just rinsing your hands with water enables many germs to remain on your hands and when you eat, you can get them into your stomach, which might make you sick. So please go back to the bathroom and wash your hands with warm water *and* soap."

This little lecture irritated Jasmine. She knew that after she washed her hands with just water, she couldn't feel or see any germs. So why did she have to use soap also? Also she noticed that her mother had made liver and onions for dinner. Ugh! Liver and onions were among her least favorite foods. Only fish of any kind and something called *osso buco* were worse.

Why couldn't Chacha make spaghetti with meatballs or pizza, or cheeseburgers with fries or hot dogs in rolls like Pilata's mother made?

After washing her hands with soap and water, Jasmine returned to the table and sat down.

Caesar had put away the newspaper and had helped Chacha put the dishes and silverware on the dining room table. Then Chacha went into the kitchen and brought the first course: a steaming bowl of freshly made vegetable soup. When everyone had eaten the vegetable soup, Chacha brought the used dishes back into the kitchen, and brought out a platter of liver and onions, a bowl of steamed broccoli, and a bowl of mashed potatoes. Of all the vegetables in the world, Chacha had to make broccoli? Why not fries with ketchup, why not macaroni and cheese, thought Jasmine. Those were vegetables too weren't they?

Dessert consisted of apples, pears, and some dry cookies called *biscotti*. Where were the goodies such as ice cream, chocolate cake, and pudding with whipped cream that normal families have for dessert? Apples and pears were merely health foods, thought Jasmine. And the biscotti, wasn't that the stuff you gave to babies when they were teething? Ugh! What a lousy dinner!

It was seven thirty when dinner was over. Jasmine asked if she could go across the street to visit with Pilata and her brother Pilatus. "Have you done your homework yet?" asked Caesar. Jasmine thought for a moment. The truth was that she hadn't done her homework yet. She had to write a 300 word composition on the subject *My Favorite Things.* She thought that this was a boring subject since her favorite things were things you weren't supposed to admit like *not* going to school, *not* having to eat liver and onions, *not* having to do homework, *not* washing her hair and so on. But if she wrote all this down, her parents and teachers would think that she was an ungrateful child, perhaps in need of better behavior training. And among her friends everyone knew about BEBE and being sent there was worse than anything. No one she knew had actually been to BEBE but all her friends knew of someone who had been sent there for being too difficult. For example Pilata claimed that her cousin's third best friend had been sent to BEBE for shaving her poor cat using her father's electric razor. Dorvit's friend knew of a girl who was sent to BEBE because she put ants in her brother's shoes. Jasmine didn't want to get into trouble with Caesar by telling a lie. So Jasmine told Caesar the truth that she hadn't yet done her homework but that she would do it in the morning between brushing her teeth and eating her breakfast. "No siree!!" said her father. "You'll do your homework tonight before going to bed. It is a bad idea to make time for fun before doing carrying out your responsibilities. There is a country called Sao Rico where the people live according to a philosophy called *mañana*. *Mañana* means *tomorrow* in Spanish and the people of Sao Rico put everything off until tomorrow in order to party today. Instead of going to work, they eat, drink, dance, play, have parades, surf and have cookouts all the time. Everything is put off until *mañana* and, of course, *mañana* never comes. So you know what happens in Sao Rico because of *mañana*? There are no vegetables because the farmers party instead of growing things. There are no schools because the teachers are on the beach having cookouts. Why you can't even buy soap in Sao Rico because the soap factories are closed. Aren't you lucky that you don't live in Sao Rico Jasmine?"

Sao Rico sounds like my kind of place thought Jasmine. *I wonder where it is and how to get there?* She hoped that her father couldn't read her mind because he wouldn't have liked what she was thinking. To her the people of Sao Rico had found the secret of life: have fun all the time! Here in Lalaville grown-ups did nothing but work and expected their kids to do the same. In the winters the fathers were always plowing the snow off the driveways with their noisy snow blowers and the mothers were always shopping, cleaning, and cooking. In the summers the fathers were always cutting the grass with their noisy little tractors and the   mothers were always shopping, cleaning, and cooking. Why not leave the snow alone so that you play and roll around in it? Why not let the grass grow so that when it got tall enough you could play hide-go-seek?

But Jasmine didn't want to fight with her father. She knew that he would not tolerate her not doing her homework. So she resigned herself to writing the stupid composition. Besides she didn't want to be the only kid in class who hadn't done her homework. She could image what might happen tomorrow in class if she came without her composition. "Jasmine, would you please come to the front of the class and read your composition," Miss Acapela would say. And what would be Jasmine's excuse for not having her composition? "I can't read it Miss Acapela because after I wrote it Bijou, my dog, ate it." Jasmine didn't have a dog and even if she had she wouldn't call it Bijou. Maybe she could say, "I can't read it Miss Acapela because after I wrote it Jarvis, my brother, ate it." Jasmine didn't have a brother either and even if she did would anyone believe that her brother ate paper? And, anyway, who would give a child a name like Jarvis? Nope, it seemed that the only reasonable course of action was to go up to her room and write the stupid composition.

3. Jasmine does her homework

Once she entered her room the first thing that Jasmine did was to close the door. Once the door was closed Jasmine felt that she was the queen of all that she could see. On the bed was her faithful and obedient doll Sochi who would give her life for Jasmine—at least that's what Jasmine thought. In the closet there were other, lesser, dolls with such names Amy, Beth, Casa, Delmore, Edith, Fatima, Goethe, Helen, Ina, Jewel, Kitty, Leslie, Mesme, Nancy, Opal, Pearl, Quinn, Rachel, Terry, Uma, Violet, Walla, Xtra, Yvette, and Zennifer.

On the wall there were pictures she had drawn using the PAINT program on her little computer. There was a large picture of Jacksnap the superdoll that Sochi liked so much. Jacksnap wore a leather jacket, which on the back said DOLLS ARE NOT SISSIES. Jasmine had her own little television but she could watch only certain programs that her parents did not censor. There was also a little desk with a nice lamp on it and a cup that held pens and pencils. Above the desk were framed certificates that gave proof that Jasmine was an outstanding young lady. One certificate was for outstanding penmanship; another was for completing two years of piano lessons; a third was for having a perfect attendance record in school. But the certificate that Jasmine was the proudest of was the one shown below.

First Place Spelling Bee Award to Jasmine Turmalina
for corectly speling
calaboose

Jasmine loved this certificate and looked at it several times each day. Image being able to spell *calaboose* without ever having seen that word before; her friend Dorvit who had also entered the contest but had won second place because she spelled *calaboose* as c-a-l-l-a-b-o-o-s-e whereas Pilata, who won third place, spelled calaboose as k-a-l-a-b-o-o-s. Still there was something about the certificate that struck Jasmine as odd. She couldn't figure out exactly what it was but she was sure that one day she would find out why.

Sochi meanwhile was unhappy because she feared that Jasmine was going to give her a bath. Sochi didn't mind being clean but the water got into her stuffing and took a long time to dry. When her stuffing was wet, Sochi was cold even under the blanket. When Sochi heard Jasmine say that there was no time for a bath today because Jasmine had to write a composition, she was very happy. In fact she was so happy she let out a little glurp. But Jasmine never heard it or at least made believe she never heard it in order not to embarrass Sochi.

Finally Jasmine sat down at her desk and took out some paper and a pencil. After collecting her thoughts she began to write. All the time she was writing she never heard Sochi singing to herself. About an hour later Jasmine put down her pencil and wiped the sweat from her brow. She had finished the composition and was quite happy with it. Here is what Jasmine wrote:

My favorite things
By
Jasmine Turmalina

It is important to have favorite things. If you don't have favorite things then you don't know what you want to have. If you only know the things you hate then you know what to avoid but you don't know what you would like. That's why it is important to have favorite things. So here is a list of some of my favorite things:
Favorite season: summer.
Favorite foods: hot dogs and spaghetti.
Favorite vegetables: French fries and ketchup.
Favorite doll and best friend: Sochi.
Favorite crawling thing: caterpillars.
Favorite small animal: scrapula.
Favorite country: Sao Rico

Favorite second best friend: Dorvit.
Favorite third best friend: Pilata.
Favorite activity: winning first prize at a spelling bee.
Favorite female parent: my mother
Favorite male parent: my father.
Favorite teacher: Miss Acapela.
Favorite things to do at home: explore the back yard.
Favorite boy to tease: Pilatus (Pilata's younger brother).
Favorite philosophy: maniana. (that's how mañana sounds)
So now you know what my favorite things are. As I get older I am sure that I will have more favorite things. For example my parents like wine and I tasted it once but I hated it. Maybe it will become one of my favorite things. Another time, at a party at our house, every grownup was eating these little crackers with some black stuff on it. My parents called it Beluga caviar and all these grown-ups were going ooh and aah about how good it was. So I came down from my room and ate one of those crackers with the black stuff on it and right away I threw up. But maybe when I get real old these crackers with the black things—they look like little spider egg sacks—will become one of my favorite things but I doubt it. But there is one thing that I know for sure will never be one of my favorite things and that is <u>boys</u>. They are silly and show off all the time and are mean to all the girls at school. Boys: never, never, never a favorite thing.

4. Jasmine explores the garden at night

When Jasmine had finished writing her composition and re-read it several times more the only doubt left in her mind was whether to add one more *never* in the phrase *Boys: never ,never, never a favorite thing.* If she did it would then read *Boys: never, never, never, never a favorite thing.* This way Miss Acapela would know how strongly Jasmine felt about this matter. "Oh well!" she said to herself, "I guess I can always make up my mind in the morning. It would only require putting in one extra word. I'm sure that I'll have time to do that!" Writing such a long composition had made Jasmine tired, hungry and thirsty. So she put on her pajamas, (but left her cap on) put her clothes under the bed (she was too tired to hang them up), put her feet into the pink rabbit slippers (that she hated) and walked down into the kitchen to see what was in the fridge. There was leftover liver and onions, garlicky salad, different kinds of smelly cheeses, a half bottle of wine, apples, pears, tomatoes, a whole bin of sweet potatoes, spinach, and broccoli a container of milk, leftover apple pie and many things in bowls with covers on top. She settled on milk and the apple pie. To make the milk more flavorful she added a half cup of chocolate syrup to it and stirred the mixture for about three minutes so that the chocolate milk, for that is what the milk and the chocolate syrup had become, would be all even. Then she sat down at the kitchen table and ate the apple pie and drank the chocolate milk. She put the used dishes in the sink and walked into the family room where she saw Caesar and Chacha watching a television program. What do grown-ups watch on TV she wondered. She heard the guy on the screen say, "Today the dollar fell against the Euro but moved up on the yen." It didn't make any sense to her at all. I mean could a dollar bill actually fall down and then move up onto something called a "yen". It was time to say goodnight. "Goodnight all," she said and started to walk up the stairs to her room. "Come give us a kiss," her parents said. So Jasmine was forced to return to the living room and hug each of her parents and endure their kisses. When this routine, which was repeated every night, was over, Jasmine finally walked up the stairs to her room. "Move over Sochi," she said. "It's time to get under the covers and get some sleep." Sochi, who had dozed off and had been dreaming of Jacksnap, was annoyed at being woken. On the other hand there was no mention by Jasmine of going out in the middle of the night to visit the hollow maple tree, so maybe Jasmine forgot all about it. This made Sochi very happy.

Jasmine put Sochi under the covers. Then she kicked off her rabbit slippers and went under the blanket next to Sochi. "Goodnight dear Sochi," she said. To which Sochi answered

"Goodnight Jasmine." The next thing you knew they were both asleep.

Jasmine fell into a deep sleep. She dreamt that there were llamas by her bedside and that she had a silly conversation with them. She dreamt that she kept a diary and that she recorded her adventure with the llamas in her diary:

One night I woke while in my bed
To face a pair of llamas.
The one was white, the other red
And wearing my pajamas.

"I'd planned ahead," the red one said
To find some clothes for llamas.
But tried instead, with lots of dread
To wear a dress of mama's."

I looked the llamas in the eye
And said you sound so silly,
For beasts like you, whate'er they try,
Go naked willy-nilly.

They asked for something good to chew
To soothe their injured pride.
I thought a moment what to do,
Then I to them replied.

"I'll feed you neither fat nor lean.
I cannot cast you candies.
It's time to stop this sorry scene.
Go home and climb the Andes!"

That night there was a full moon, and all was silent in the back yard. Well that's not exactly true. All was *almost* silent in the back yard. If you listened carefully you could hear the snoring of the scrapulas, the wiggling of the caterpillars, the hooting of the owls, the digging of the moles, and... *what was that?* There was a strange sound and it seemed to be coming from the hollow maple tree. It sounded like Whee-er-yoo...Whee-er-yoo..., almost like *where are you*!

Jasmine and the llamas

Jasmine was the first to hear it. She rubbed her eyes and wondered if she was still dreaming. But then she saw the light of the moon coming through the window and she heard Sochi's gentle breathing. Sochi's head was halfway under the pillow and she was drooling. *Well maybe it was a dream*, thought Jasmine. But then she heard it again Whee-er-yoo...Whee-er-yoo. This was no dream! She gave Sochi a gentle push and said, "There is something going on in the yard. We need to find out what it is. Remember our promise to Optimus and Hypolux that we would find what was making such strange noises in the maple tree! Come on! Get up!"

Sochi nearly fainted with fear when she heard these words. "I can't go!" She cried, "I have a toothache, a stomachache, a fly in my eye, a bad rash on my behind, a fever and a sore throat. The nails on my feet are falling off and my nose is stuffed. I swallowed my tongue and got my finger stuck in my nose. There is no way that I can go with you!" When she heard all these complaints Jasmine laughed, "Dolls don't get fevers or sore throats," she said. "They also don't get rashes on their behinds. You're just afraid of going into the garden with me in the middle of the night. What's the worst that can happen? If we meet Waxface I can protect you because Waxface is no danger to humans. If we run into the Tilops we'll tell them that there's nothing they can steal from us since we won't be carrying any valuables. Anyway we know the kind of tricks the Tilops like to pull and we'll be on guard. "What about the Craxies?' moaned Sochi. "Not even you can protect us from the Craxies!"

The Craxies could be a problem thought Jasmine. On the other hand she had never seen a Craxie and none of her friends had either. She had heard, however, of the mischief that Craxies could make, from articles in the newspaper that her father had read to her. Only last week her father had lectured her about the dangers of going out at night into the garden without adult supervision. *Let me read you this* he had said. Caesar then proceeded to read an article from the **Lalaville Chronicle** whose headline said:

Craxies strike in the heart of Lalaville

Boy smeared with paint

Lalaville, April 10—In a news conference called by police chief Donohue, he warned parents to make sure that their small children did not go out in the middle of the night by themselves. He cited the example Michael Pollux, aged nine, who went out into the garden at three o'clock in the morning to look for his shoe, which he had misplaced earlier that evening in a shoe throwing contest with his friends Lenny Dioscuri, and Robert Castor. As Michael told the police: *I put my foot on this rock and before I knew it I was glued fast to the rock. A few minutes later these rabbit-like things with frog legs ran over with paint brushes and started to paint me. They painted my head blue, my arms green, and my legs yellow with polka dots. When they were finished one of them yelled Craxies Forever and then they vanished. Meanwhile all these animals came over and laughed their heads off! I yelled for help but my parents didn't hear. By six this morning the glue had loosened and I went back into the house. When my mother saw me she screamed for help. I guess she didn't recognize me. My father yelled "get away, get away you Technicolor bandit or I'll set our dog on you." I knew there was nothing to be afraid of because our dog is a dwarf poodle that is afraid of his own shadow. Finally they recognized that I was their son and they called the police.*

Chief Donohue said that there are too many disobedient children in Lalaville and that's why there were so many Craxies around.

Common you people!! the chief had said. *Get your kids to behave so that the Craxies will go to other places like Lutherville, or even Deltaville!*

A craxie

So apparently the Craxies do exist, thought Jasmine. *Well too bad! We'll just have to take our chances!* she said to give herself more courage.

Jasmine put on her blue jeans, a red sweater, and white sneakers. She dressed Sochi in a little leather jacket, a pair of little purple booties, and a yellow beret. She then quietly made her bed and carried Sochi down to the kitchen. Once in the kitchen she opened the door to the pantry and removed a can of sardines and made herself a sardine sandwich, which she stuffed into her pocket. Then she closed the pantry door very, very, quietly and took a deep breath. *This is it* she said to Sochi. She looked at the kitchen clock; it said two thirty in the morning. Then she quietly opened the back door leading to the yard and walked out. She closed the back door very slowly behind her to avoid making any noise.

She and Sochi were now all alone in the yard. She couldn't even get back into the house because the kitchen door had locked behind her.

The Whee-er-yoo sound she had heard before was gone. Everything was now super quiet. The light from the moon that fell through the branches of the trees appeared on the ground like yellow little jigsaw pieces. Here and there one could see a slowly moving little green snake looking for something to eat. Some of the flowers had folded up their petals to keep out the night cold. Suddenly Jasmine heard the Hoot! Hoot! of an owl. Then she heard the squeaking of a mouse running across the yard and the flapping of the wings of a large bird that she figured was the owl. This was followed by more squeaking and a loud shriek. Then once again all was quiet. Jasmine shivered. *Maybe it wasn't such a great idea to go out at night in a place where owls and snakes were on the prowl*, she thought. *How big did these owls get anyway?* she thought. She realized that owls were no threat since she had never heard of an owl flying off with a little girl, not even a doll. The little green snakes were too small to be a problem and she had learned in school that they had no teeth and were not poisonous.

Jasmine was maybe fifty feet from the hollow maple when Sochi began to fidget. "What is it Sochi?" she asked. "Don't you hear it," whispered Sochi. "It's coming from that corner of the yard." At first Jasmine heard nothing. Then slowly, almost like a soft fog, a beautiful and haunting tune wafted across the yard and reached her ears. "Wow," thought Jasmine, "this tune is almost as good as my favorite song *Little Girls Need to Dance*.

The song *Little Girls Need to Dance* was a great favorite with girls in the age group six to twenty four. It was sung by a fifty-six year old man who had very long hair and called himself *Prince Groïser Yukel*. The most popular lines in the song went like this:

> *Little girls like to dance*
> *On a bridge in the south of France*
> *One step left and one step right*
> *Dance all day and dance all night.*

However this tune was different. It went something like this:

> *Samkhaya Yoga Dhyana Yoga*
> *Gnyama Karma Sanyasa Yoga*
> *Karma Sanyasa Yoga*
> *Gnyana Vignana Yoga*

Yes it was beautiful! Jasmine had once seen a group of bald Asian people dressed in red robes that sang like that. Jasmine and Sochi began to walk to the corner of the yard where the music was coming from. Sochi began to hum the tune. "Faster! Faster! Let's get there faster! " said Sochi.

For some reason Jasmine became afraid. *I don't like this,* she thought. *No nice person should be out in the yard at this time of night playing such a strange tune.*

Then the playing stopped!

5. Jasmine confronts Waxface

As they quietly walked on the soft moss and young grass of the yard, the moon rose up further in the sky and a pale light fell on the corner of the yard. There, stood a creature about three feet tall with a completely round head made of wax (hence the name Waxface) and a red wattle hanging under his chin. The creature had no hair and was dressed in a green suit, the kind that you see on leprechauns. It stood on turkey legs and had very short arms. The turkey feet were encased in a very expensive pair of shoes. In one hand it had a flute; in the other it had a sack. The sack was bulging with things that moved. When Jasmine and Sochi saw Waxface they were very frightened by his appearance. As soon as Waxface saw Jasmine and Sochi he began playing the flute. Sochi became very agitated when she heard the music. She took off her jacket, ripped off her purple booties, and flung her yellow beret to the ground. "Other dolls wear Gucci, Chanel, Valentino, and Lord & Taylor and I have to wear these hand-me-downs from your other dolls. I want to go with Waxface! I don't want Waxface to see me in these rags!" she screamed. Jasmine knew that Sochi had temporarily gone crazy. She had heard of the effect that Waxface's music had on dolls. But Sochi was her best friend. It was her duty to save Sochi from herself.

Jasmine approached Waxface. "Please stop your flute playing," she said. "As you can see it disturbs my best friend and number one doll Sochi." "Let me go, let me go!" cried Sochi. "I love Mr. Waxface. I want to go with this beautiful creature and devote myself to him. I want to cook his meals, wash his clothes, and clean his house. You have no right to keep me against my will. I know my constitutional rights!"

Did dolls have constitutional rights? thought Jasmine. She had heard about the United States Constitution in school and in fact she and other students in her class had written up a *class* constitution with the following articles:

Articles of the Constitution of Miss Acapela's class

1. All students have the right of free assembly outside class.
2. All students have the right of free speech outside class.
3. All students have the right to a 15 minute recess in the morning.
4. All students have the right to a 15 minute recess in the afternoon.
5. All students have the right to have as many friends as they want.
6. All girl students have the right to hate boys.
7. All students have the right to trade their lunches with others.
8. All students have the right to pursue happiness within the school grounds.
9. All students have the right to petition to amend this constitution.

Was there such a constitution like that for dolls? Certainly not! decided Jasmine. And even if there was, Jasmine had to protect her friend from this dollnapper. The haunting tune that Waxface played had made Sochi blind to how ugly he really was.

"I am your protector and friend," said Jasmine to Sochi. "Before I let you go with Mr. Waxface let's find out what his plans are for you. And stop trying to escape. Remember, I can put you in my closet if I want to and choose one of the other dolls to be my best friend."

When Sochi heard this strong warning from her owner, she had the bitterest feelings ever against Jasmine. There was nothing in the world that she wanted as much as going with Waxface. She felt that life with Waxface would be endless days of fun, eating Italian ice cream, having red balloons, never having to take a bath, wearing fancy clothes from Gucci, Chanel, Valentino, and Lord & Taylor, and other wonderful treats that Jasmine didn't provide. But she knew that Jasmine was a tough boss and she definitely didn't want to end up in the closet if she couldn't get to go with Waxface. So she tried to keep her mouth shut and her agitation to a minimum.

Waxface could speak but because his head was made of wax, his mouth could only move slowly. The result was that when he spoke the words were dragged out. For example if he said *I am hungry* it came out *Iyeyeye aamm huuunngggrrry*. It was very annoying to have to listen to him and Jasmine hoped that he would talk in short sentences. Besides it wasn't pretty watching the reddish wattle shake beneath his mouth when he spoke.

[Reader: We shall not try to imitate the way Waxface actually talked. We shall only give the content of what he said.]

Waxface had stopped playing the flute. He looked at Jasmine with small, greasy, eyes. Jasmine has observed that part of Waxface's ear had melted. She wondered if she inserted a wick into his waxy head Waxface would become a giant candle.

Jasmine looked at the sack that Waxface was carrying. She could see the moving bulges in the sack. "What have you got there Mr. Waxface?" she asked. Waxface was being coy. "What, you mean this sack here? Why that's just my dinner my dear! Even though I don't look like ordinary people I still have to eat, you know. Look at my short arms, my thin legs, and my short stature. Without food, my legs would get skinnier, and my arms even shorter. Like all living creatures, I must eat to stay alive."

Now that Waxface wasn't playing the flute, Sochi began to emerge from her obsession. "Don't believe him, Jasmine," she whispered. "I think that he's got dolls in the sack, dolls that he probably dollnapped this very night. He probably plans to eat them."

Two views of Waxface: On the left he is looking around for dolls to kidnap. On the right he is seen playing his flute.

Jasmine stood as tall as she could. She looked down at Waxface and said: "Look Mr. Waxface I have no intention of giving you my doll Sochi here. Zip! Nada! Pas de chance! Also it seems to me that you are trespassing on private property and if you don't behave and leave when I tell you to leave I shall call the authorities!" The problem was that Jasmine didn't know what authorities to call. Should it be the police? Or maybe the fire department? Or maybe even the Animal Society? "Do you think for one minute that I'm going to let you eat Sochi here or any of the dolls you probably have in your sack?"

"Thataway Jasmine," Sochi whispered. "Show him that I'm not afraid!" Then she retreated as far as she could under Jasmine's red sweater.

The truth was that Waxface did need to eat to stay alive but, of course, he didn't eat dolls. His favorite meals consisted of apple cores and banana peels and walnut shells. His favorite drink was Dr. Brown's diet cream soda. Sometimes when he was hungry for a snack he would sneak into movie houses and eat the popcorn and candies that fell to the floor from the hands of small children.

"Look," Waxface said. "Before you do anything rash, young lady, let me tell you my story. You will see, my dear, that my soul is not nearly as ugly as this bodily package that fate has imprisoned me in. Moreover those rumors that I sell dolls to pirates in the Arabian Sea are pure bunk. I would never do such a thing! Those rumors were started by certain people in Washington, D.C. to discredit me! "

Then with great difficulty Waxface sat down on a rock and began telling his story. Before Jasmine started listening she told herself that she would never sit on that rock again.

6. Waxface tells his story

Here is the story that Waxface told Jasmine and Sochi. We have left out some inappropriate details that would frighten younger readers and disgust older ones.

In 1956, the Cooperson family was celebrating the Thanksgiving holiday in its spacious, rent-controlled, apartment at 1350 Shakespeare Avenue in the Bronx, New York. The dinner table had been set with all the usual Thanksgiving new-world goodies including turkey, chicken wings, corn, sweet potatoes, nachos, hot and sour soup, gefilte fish etc. To make the Thanksgiving dinner a really festive occasion, Mrs. Cooperson placed wax candles in silver candlesticks along the long table where 36 dinner guests and family sat to enjoy the feast. As everyone said later *This was the best Thanksgiving diner party they ever attended.* At about seven-thirty that evening Mrs. Cooperson and her daughters Merrill, Beryl, and Felicia cleared the table and threw all the leftovers in a large plastic bag. They also removed all the left-over wax from the candlesticks and threw that into the same plastic bag. Then Mr. Cooperson and his friends Herrick and Dryden carried the bag into the alley between 1348 and 1350 Shakespeare Avenue where, on the coming Wednesday, the garbage men would pick up the trash. Later that evening there was a violent lightning storm and a one-billion volt lightning bolt struck the bag. The tremendous energy melted the wax and fused all the items in the bag together. For some unknown reason the lightning bolt gave life to the ghastly mess inside the bag. This is how Waxface came to be.

In the first few hours after his creation, Waxface took stock of his situation. He removed all the excess items from his body such as paper napkins, toothpicks, chicken bones, uneaten Chinese fortune cookies, and pieces of pumpkin pie. Pretty soon he became more functional and his appearance improved. At first glance he looked like a common elf with an abnormally large head.

Life for Waxface was difficult at first. He got a job in a toy store called *Friends of Tots* but things were not going well. Children screamed when they saw him. At Christmas the management tried to dress him up as one of Santa's elves but they couldn't hide his turkey legs and the children screamed even more. *Don't take me to that elf with the turkey legs and the wax head* they would cry. Waxface slept among the dolls in the store. One night when he couldn't sleep he passed the time by playing a tune on a flute that had been imported from Zanzibar. Then something fantastic happened: all the dolls came to life and started coming to Waxface. At first he was frightened but then he saw that the dolls meant him no harm. In fact it was the opposite: some dolls brought him apple cores and banana peels, other dolls brought him walnut shells and still other dolls brought him Dr. Brown's diet cream soda. As long as he played his flute the dolls were ecstatic (crazy in love) about him. Some made him clothes, others polished his waxy head and still others trimmed the talons on his turkey feet.

Unfortunately the managers of the store decided to fire Waxface because children were afraid of him and children were their most important customers. Another reason they fired him was that the New York City Fire Department declared him to be a fire hazard, being made of wax and all. It was a difficult decision for the managers because they had grown fond of him. He may have been ugly and a fire hazard but he had a certain style that they liked. One manager called him a *boulevardier.*[1] Actually Waxface was quite likable. If you could avoid looking at his red wattle while he spoke and

---

[1] A boulevardier is a well-dressed gentleman in France that people admire for his style, wit, and clothes. Boulevardiers are often seen walking the broad streets of Paris called boulevards. That's why they are called boulevardiers. Anyone who has style and wit can be called a boulevardier.

listen patiently to what he had to say you would find that he was full of good ideas.

When Waxface was fired Heather and Hilton, two dolls that were crazy about him, decided to go with him. After weeks of walking the streets, Waxface was ready to melt down. He hadn't found a new job, he was terribly hungry, and he was worried about having to take responsibility for Heather and Hilton. During the day Waxface stayed out of sight, usually in the upper branches of a tree. He hated it when little children would look at him and make turkey-type Goble...Goble noises at him. Some of the smaller kids would scream in terror when they saw him and stopped their crying only when their mothers or nannies reassured them by making up a story that Waxface was O.K and looked the way he did because he worked for the circus as "Turkey Man". To avoid the ridicule and fear that followed him during the day, Waxface would come out only at night. Eventually most people forgot about him.

Then one evening life for Waxface changed. At about midnight, a tired and hungry Waxface could be seen dragging Heather and Hilton by his short arms near Riverside Drive in Manhattan. Suddenly an elegantly dressed couple came near. The man was dressed in a tuxedo, black tie, and top hat and the woman wore a long white gown and a diamond necklace. They were returning from a party where they had been celebrated for being very rich. Both had had too much wine to drink and couldn't focus their eyes very well. When they saw Waxface they said "Young, er, whatever you are, are those two things that you are holding by your short arms dolls?" Waxface was startled to realize that they were speaking to him. "Yes," he said. "Those dolls are under my care and their names are Heather and Hilton. "Well," the couple said, "we are doll collectors and we would like to buy them from you. Would the sum of er...five thousand dollars be enough to purchase them?" Waxface couldn't believe what his ears had heard. What a fantastic offer! Here was a golden opportunity to get some money to buy clothes, food, and a good pair of shoes specially designed for his turkey feet. "Why yes," he said, "I'll let you have Heather and Hilton on condition that you don't eat them!"

Five thousand dollars for a pair of dolls was of course a ridiculously large offer. But remember this couple was ultra rich and they were drunk. You could say that Waxface had won the lottery!

As it turned out the rich couple had no plans to eat Heather and Hilton. The rich couple preferred to eat tiny, shiny, fish eggs and rotten cheese from France. They drank a kind of spoiled grape juice called sherry. Their plans for Heather and Hilton were to cover them in blue porcelain and sell them as art pieces imported from Holland. Heather and Hilton were rather silly dolls anyway and didn't mind. They ended up living in a large apartment on Park Avenue with a little girl whose name was Fortuna. Fortuna was nice enough but she had a really stupid dog called Faunus who sniffed Heather and Hilton all day long. He didn't know what to make of them. Heather and Hilton lived in fear that Faunus would use them the way dogs use fire hydrants.

Meanwhile Waxface had found his calling in life. During the day he slept in treetops or deep bushes and at night he went around with a large plastic bag and his flute. When he played his flute dolls would awaken and try to come to him. Of course it wasn't easy for the dolls to get to him since they were inside the house and he was outside in the yard. If you looked carefully you could see hundreds of dolls banging on the inside of bedroom windows, clamoring to get to him. Sometimes, when the windows were open, like in the spring or summer, the dolls could get to him by throwing themselves out of the windows like lemmings[2].

Once Waxface collected his dolls he would go to one of several doll markets where dolls were bought and sold. His favorite doll market was in the great train station in New York City called Grand Central Station where trains came and went from all over the suburbs. There he could get a good price for his dolls, sometimes as much as five dollars for each one. Once he sold his dolls, he went to an all-night Korean grocery store in the borough of Queens to buy apple cores, banana peels, and walnut shells. Mr. Parks, who was the owner of the store, had made a deal with Waxface that he would provide all the cores, peels and shells that Waxface needed for his diet for fifty dollars a week. To get the apple cores, banana peals and walnut shells, Mr. Parks kept some special animals in the basement: five hamsters and rabbits that ate apples but left the cores behind; two chimpanzees that ate bananas but left the peels behind; and four squirrels that ate the inside of the walnuts but left the shells behind. Mr. Parks's son Kim was in charge of keeping the basement clean and collecting all the items left behind by the animals. Kim

---

[2] Lemmings are similar to mice and live in the artic regions of the world. They have a tendency to fling themselves into the ocean from high cliffs leading to their destruction.

was not a happy young man; he often thought of running away and joining the army.

Occasionally bullies would play cruel tricks on Waxface. The worst of these tricks were done by two very bad boys Frank Fallon and John Tyson. One night Fallon and Tyson were throwing empty cans and bottles at squirrels and rabbits in Central Park[3]. As it happened Waxface was just returning from having bought provisions from Mr. Parks. When he saw what Fallon and Tyson were doing he forgot who he was, and how weak he was compared to humans, and yelled at them to stop. When Fallon and Tyson saw that his head was made of wax, they grabbed him, put a wick near his ear and lit it. Then they ran away. Fortunately one of the rabbits saw what happened and came and blew out the flame on the wick. Waxface was not seriously hurt but a small part of his ear had melted away.

Despite his horrible appearance, Waxface was not a bad creature. When he sold the dolls that he dollnapped he got written promises from the buyers that the dolls would not be harmed. Waxface never sold his dolls to the Gorgons, foe example, who were known to remove the stuffing of the dolls to make pillows for the Inuits[4]. The Inuits lived in igloos made of ice and needed soft pillows to rest their heads when they went to sleep. Once the stuffing was removed from the dolls, the dolls lost track of their *inner selves*, so to speak, and were of little use to anyone.

Waxface didn't do business with the Sirens either. After acquiring their dolls, the Sirens sold them to the Pandora Circus company. The Pandora Circus company was run by the evil Dr. Priam and was a horrible place to work in. The circus animals fought among each other, most people walked around with sore throats and colds, and the high wire artists frequently fell-off and broke their arms and/or legs or worse. The bearded lady's beard wouldn't grow and "the world's strongest man" had grown so weak he needed a cane just to walk. Dr. Priam operated many game booths where people could win dolls by knocking over pins with a bowling ball, or shooting plastic ducks with a BB gun, or guessing how many jelly beans were in a jar. The dolls had a miserable time in the Pandora Circus Company. They sat on these shelves all day and had to wait for some customer to win them by being successful in the game booth. It was a very

---

[3] A large park in New York City.
[4] Also known as Eskimos.

humiliating process. For example just when a doll thought that she was going to get picked by some young guy who shot the ducks, the guy's girlfriend would say *Not that one—it's too ugly. Get me the one with the blonde hair.* Imagine how that made the rejected doll feel!

This was essentially Waxface's story. When he had finished telling it he took out a can of Dr. Brown's diet cream soda, flipped open the tab and drank the whole can in a single swallow. If you looked carefully, you could see a single tear running down his greasy cheek.

7. Jasmine and Waxface reconcile

When Jasmine heard Waxface's story, she felt sorry for him. She recognized that ugly as he was, he was the possessor of a gentle soul. Imagine, she thought to herself, what life must be like when you have a head of wax, the legs of a turkey, a turkey wattle under your chin, and a stature of only three feet. And yet Waxface cared about the dolls that he dollnapped. He tried his best to find places for the dolls where they wouldn't be harmed. Of course dollnapping was a bad business. You couldn't just go and take people's dolls without permission! On the other hand how was Waxface to live? Would a bank give him a job as a bank teller? Certainly not! Banks can be very warm places and can you image the reaction of a customer when they see Waxface dribbling wax all over the money he or she is depositing? Would a grocery store allow him to be a cashier? Out of the question! Waxface was too short to reach the cash register and didn't have the strength to put the food items into a bag. Could Waxface become a policeman? Ridiculous! What self respecting criminal would be afraid of Waxface? Could Waxface become a lawyer? Perhaps! But Waxface spoke so slowly (remember that his lips were made of wax and moved very slowly) that he could never be effective before a jury. Imagine Waxface addressing the jury as:

Memmmbersss offf the juuurryy: I wwiilll shooww that myyy cliiieentt iss nnoott gguilllltty off the criimmme that hheee iisss aaccusssedd offf.

Moreover even with a carefully tailored suit and a specially designed set of shoes to hide his talons, Waxface would still look funny to the jurors. His red wattle was difficult to hide with a tie. His bald wax head could be covered with a hat but hats were not allowed in the courtroom. Also courtrooms were very hot places because witnesses and lawyers in their careful explications generated a lot of hot air. Jasmine had this image of

Waxface arguing his case before a jury while his nose began melting. Ugh! It was too horrible to think about!

While Jasmine was having all these thoughts, Sochi peeked out from under Jasmine's red sweater. "Hit him with a rock," she urged. "Beat him with a stick," she whispered. "Throw sand into his eyes," she begged. "Shush Sochi!" Jasmine warned. "Let me think for a moment." Hearing these words, Sochi gave Jasmine a dirty look and retreated in Jasmine's sweater.

The story that Waxface told left out one important thing and Jasmine now realized what it was: Waxface was supremely lonely. That was probably why he got into the dollnapping business in the first place. It was true that the dollnapping served Waxface's purpose namely to have something to sell so that he could get some money to buy the needed food from Mr. Parks. But surely Waxface could have gotten his apple cores and banana peels from scavenging the garbage cans that had been placed all over the city[5]. Walnut shells were easily gotten from the trash baskets outside the Museum of Modern Art because many of the tourists who visited that museum loved eating walnuts. It made them feel less like tourists and more like New Yorkers. So why did Waxface turn to dollnapping? Because, Jasmine realized, he was lonely and the dolls—at least until he sold them—were his friends.

Waxface's situation now became clear to Jasmine. But what to do? While she was thinking of a solution to Waxface and his dollnapping addiction she felt a tapping under her sweater: it was Sochi. "Are you going to stand there doing nothing while he plans to murder us?" she hissed as she stuck her head out. Jasmine finally lost her patience. "Sochi: one more word out of you while I'm thinking and you will cease to be my number one doll. I will find some comfortable corner in the closet for you and visit you once a year—maybe on St. Valentine's Day!"

These words terrified Sochi. For now she would have to remain quiet. But some day, some day...she would get her revenge. Annoyed as she was, Sochi had no choice but to crawl back under Jasmine's sweater.

---

[5] At the time that this story is told the mayor of New York City was very keen on having a clean city and had garbage cans installed everywhere where people gathered.

Meanwhile an idea was coming to Jasmine. Although she often didn't listen to conversations that took place at the dinner table, preoccupied as she was with Dorvit's treachery in gossiping about her at school, there was something that her father had said that caught her ear. It was said last week when her mother, Chacha, had cooked meatballs and spaghetti and had served ice-cream for desert. Jasmine remembered it well because she had been excused from eating broccoli, which her mother had served as a vegetable. Her mother had tried to force her to eat the broccoli, pointing out that broccoli had many important vitamins that Jasmine needed to grow. But her father, Caesar, had come to her aid and had said to Chacha: *Honey it don't mean a thing if it ain't got that zing! And this broccoli ain't got no zing. Kapish?*

While eating dessert, Caesar and Chacha had been talking about investing money in the construction of a branch of the toy-store chain *Friends of Tots*. But Caesar had his doubts. "So what's the problem?" said Chacha. "Everybody likes toys and you will be making many children very happy! So why not invest?" Jasmine had heard this conversation and while she didn't know much about money or investing she knew that food and clothes didn't come free but that people were willing to give you anything you wanted as long as you gave them these little pieces of green paper called *cash*. To get these little pieces of green paper you either had to work or *invest*.

But Caesar was still unsure. "See honey here is the problem. The owners of *Friends of Tots* want to open the store in Southern California in a town called Locoloco. The people of Locoloco are unlike the people anywhere else. They wear masks, put on funny suits, shave their hair, paint their faces, grease their bodies, pierce their noses, tattoo their arms, shrink their hips, enlarge their heads, grow tails and keep chickens and turkeys as pets. They hate anyone that looks or acts normal. They have lots of money and would be happy to spend their money buying dolls because the people of Locoloco don't like other humans and prefer the company of dolls and strange creatures like themselves."

By now Jasmine had become interested in the conversation between her parents. Locoloco seemed almost as nice as Sao Rico. Why did her parents choose to live in a dull place like Lalaville she wondered?

"I still don't see what the problem is," said Chacha. "What do you care what the people of Locoloco are like. Investing money there doesn't require that we move there does it?"

"That's right," said Caesar. "But where are the owners going to find someone strange enough to run the *Friends of Tots* store in Locoloco? So far everyone that they tried to hire to run the store either hated the place or was hated by the residents of Locoloco."

That was all that Jasmine could remember of the conversation. But now, recalling what her father has said that evening, she finally knew what the solution was to Waxface and his dollnapping problem.

She moved next to Waxface and took out her handkerchief and wiped the tear that had rolled down his cheek. "Look Mr. Waxface," she said. "I'm about to make you an offer you can't refuse. If you agree to return all the dolls that you have dollnapped tonight and promise to quit your dollnapping habit I can tell you where you can find a job and a home. You will never have to dollnap again and yet you will be surrounded by dolls all day and all night long." Then Jasmine told Waxface all about Locoloco, the strange people that lived there, its location in warm sunny California where it never gets too hot, and where his strangeness would look perfectly normal and no one would make fun of him. She even gave Waxface her cell phone number and e-mail address and promised to keep in touch. Waxface was profoundly moved; no one had ever been so kind to him before. He was given a chance to make a real life for himself instead of living the life of a sewer rat. He gave Jasmine a hug with his short arms and rubbed his head into her sweater. While Jasmine was preoccupied with Waxface in this tender moment, Sochi leaned out of Jasmine's sweater and tried to kick Waxface in the ear. But her legs were too short and she didn't quite reach him. Then she quickly scrambled back under Jasmine's sweater.

Finally Jasmine gave Waxface a kiss and bid him goodbye. Since her lips were chapped, the wax that rubbed off on them was very soothing. Without another word, Waxface was gone and Jasmine and Sochi were left alone. "It's a good thing he left when he did," Sochi snarled. "I was ready to show him no mercy."

8. The Tilops ambush Jasmine

It now was very quiet. The moon had reached its highest point in the night sky and gave just enough light for Jasmine to recognize the familiar shapes in the garden. There were some daffodils here, a gravelly stone path there, two fake pink flamingos in the corner, a birdhouse hanging from the apple tree near the vegetable patch, and several bird feeders hanging off metal poles next to an old stone wall. On the far side of the stone wall the yard was largely unattended and overgrown with brambles, evergreens, and holly. Jasmine didn't like to go there even in daylight. One time she went there with her second best friend Dorvit and frightened a small red fox that had made its home in a small burrow near the *Rosa canina*[6] . Dorvit was so frightened she almost jumped out of her shoes and threatened later to downgrade Jasmine to being her third best friend. Another time she heard some squeaking and growling noise back near the thorny red berry bush and went to investigate. As she came nearer the growling became louder and she retreated back to the house. From then on she didn't go back there unless she was accompanied by Chacha or Caesar.

But now Jasmine was on the near side of the stone wall. She could make out her friend the clay screech owl, perching on a wooden post, and standing motionless while covered in white pigeon waste. It was clear that the owl, whose purpose had been to frighten away pigeons and grackles, had failed in its mission. In the middle of the yard stood a stone bowl on top of a fluted stone column anchored in a concrete base. At the bottom of the bowl was some mucky water with algae and lichen growing in it. When clean and filled with water the bowl served as a birdbath but Caesar hadn't gotten around to cleaning it yet.

There was one other place in the yard that Jasmine didn't like and was afraid of. It was the white tool shed near the gate that stood locked and mysterious during the day and appeared like a ghostly apparition at night. Once Jasmine went in there with Caesar who was looking for some tools. Inside there were millions of rusty tools, paint cans, summer furniture, brooms and rakes, and sacks of plant food, fertilizer, cement, and other things that smelled funny or gave off a lot of dust when handled. Inside the shed Caesar had asked her to fetch a small hammer that lay on a rusty metal table way in the back where it was dark even when the door to the shed was open and the sun was shining

---

[6]This bush is commonly known as the *dog rose*.

in. Jasmine had found the hammer but saw some movement and fleeting shadows in the far corner of the shed. She let out a scream and ran to Caesar's arms. Caesar hugged her but ignored her story. *It's either your overheated imagination or a field mouse that you saw,* he had said. But Jasmine was not reassured: *how could a small field mouse make such a large shadow?* She had asked. But Caesar didn't want to discuss this matter further. Pretty soon they left the shed and Caesar locked the door with a combination lock. But Jasmine saw that the door didn't close completely because the wood had warped and there was plenty of room for small or very thin creatures to go in or out.

Now, in the middle of the night, the shed looked forbidding and made Jasmine uneasy. *Did anyone live in there,* she wondered? *And if they did where they fiends or friends?*

What Jasmine had seen that time when she was in the shed with Caesar was not a product of her "overheated imagination"! The moving shadow she had glimpsed belonged to a Tilop. Several Tilops lived in the back of the shed and during the day they lived under an old wooden bench that Caesar had stored back there and covered with an oilcloth coated with linseed oil. This oilcloth protected the Tilops from bad weather, for example heavy rain. But of course it never rained inside the shed since it had a good solid roof. So you can see that if the Tilops had a weakness it was that they weren't all that smart. Because Tilops could squeeze themselves into very thin shapes they had no trouble getting in or out of the shed at night. During the day they slept but at night they came out to harass and steal from children who refused to obey their parents' orders to stay in the house and go to sleep.

Tilops were not dangerous but like pickpockets and thieves everywhere they liked to take things that didn't belong to them. Unlike Waxface, Tilops were not ugly. They were about two feet tall and looked like two-dimensional Spanish bull fighters[7]. Their heads looked like towels except that, if you looked carefully, you could see a mouth, a nose, and eyes. They were very, very thin and wore tight pants and open vests with important messages on the back. These messages were not always easy to understand by young children, even those whose fathers and mothers were very learned people. For example the Tilops that operated in Lalaville had vests with the following imprinted messages:

---

[7]Also known *as matadors.*

You can't empty the ocean with a spoon.
or
The deeper the hole the longer the fall.
or
You don't have to look up to see that it's raining.
or
A dog's size is not determined by how loud he barks.
or
There are three kinds of people: those who know how to count and those who don't.
or
Make money first. Love will come later.
or
Everybody knows where the fish store is.
or
You can't hold two watermelons in only one hand.
or
You can't sit on two horses with only one behind.
or
An old friend is better than two new ones.

Very few people had ever seen Tilops and many people, including Caesar and Chacha, didn't even believe that they existed. Those children that had been hoodwinked by the Tilops were often too embarrassed to admit it. So instead of reporting the Tilops to the police, these children simply denied having had an encounter with the Tilops.

No one knew where the Tilops came from. Tilops operated all over the world and could speak many languages. In India the Tilops spoke Hindu, in China, they spoke Chinese, in England they spoke English with a British accent and in France they spoke French. In the United States the Tilops were fatter than the Tilops in other countries. For example in India and China the Tilops were only two millimeters thick (about the thickness of two quarter coins pressed together). In France they were about three millimeters thick because of the wine that French Tilops liked to drink. But in the United States the Tilops were five millimeters thick, about the thickness of a thin pencil. The extra thickness made it difficult for American Tilops to slip under closed doors or past door jams. American Tilops could often be seen stuffing themselves on French fries left behind by children at airports. Canadian Tilops often tried to pass themselves off as American Tilops (because there were more suckers in America) but they always gave themselves away by saying things like "How would like to buy the Brooklyn Bridge, eh?" or "How about lending me your brand new bike, eh?" or "How about giving me change: two quarters for my dime, eh?" The Canadian Tilops always said "eh" at the end of every sentence because their tongues were too small for their mouths.

The Tilops

When Tilops would pull off a particularly clever stunt like selling some poor kid a single, used, smelly, sneaker in return for the kid's monthly allowance of ten dollars, they would celebrate. Usually these celebrations took place in the middle of the night. Tilops from different countries had different ways of celebrating. Tilops from Egypt would go to the top of the great pyramids and slide down in aluminum pots. Tilops in Brazil would eat piranha sandwiches using live piranhas. This was actually not such a great idea because the piranhas sometimes bit the tongues of the Brazilian Tilops with the result that they began to talk like the Canadian Tilops. Canadian Tilops would drink French wine and sing French songs, which made the French Tilops angry since the French Tilops felt that no one had the right to sing French songs unless you were French.

While Jasmine was having these disturbing thoughts about what or who was living in the shed, three of the Tilops that lived in the shed slipped past the warped shed door and quickly and quietly surrounded Jasmine. The Tilops were so thin that at first Jasmine thought that she was surrounded by three small waving towels with writings on them. Of course once the Tilops began to speak Jasmine knew that these were not towels but Tilops.

"Hello my darling little Miss," said one of the Tilops. "My name is Fleece, and these are my two friends Flimflam and Toadstool. I see that you are out for a walk this beautiful night. Very good, very good! This is your lucky day.... I mean your lucky *night*! Flimflam and I and 'Stool' here were just passing by and then we saw you and decided to come over and say hello!"

Before Fleece could continue he was interrupted by Toadstool who appeared annoyed and began to shake the way a drying shirt shakes on a clothesline in the wind. "You know I hate it when you call me 'Stool'," he said. "My name is Toadstool and that's what you call me if you want to remain my friend. I will not let the nickname 'Stool' pass from your lips without protesting!"

Meanwhile Jasmine was recovering from the shock of suddenly being surrounded by the three Tilops. When she saw how small and thin they were she quickly lost her fear and regained her composure. Based on what she had already heard of their conversation she decided that these Tilops were not all that smart and that she could probably defeat any trick that they might want to pull on her. Sochi's initial fear of the Tilops evaporated also; actually she found them rather cute especially the one called Flimflam. She could smell his after shave lotion and loved the message on his tee-shirt that said:

Two heads are better than one but not on the same person.

To Sochi, Flimflams tee-shirt message was very wise. Sochi had always had a weakness for very intelligent creatures that were also handsome. Sochi wondered how Jasmine would feel if she, Sochi, flirted a little with him and perhaps even went away with him. But this was not the time to be disloyal. If what had been said about the Tilops was true Jasmine was going to need her help in dealing with them. Sochi was proud of herself: Jasmine was lucky to have such a loyal friend.

After Fleece had apologized to Toadstool and promised never to call him 'Stool' again he turned his attention back to Jasmine. "My darling little Miss," he said. "It is never too early in life to buy *insurance*. Now you may not understand the concept of *insurance* but it is very easy to explain to a bright young Miss such as yourself. Let me illustrate with an example. I see that you have a very lovely and valuable doll that you call Sochi. Now permit me to say that Sochi is as beautiful a doll as I have seen. I am sure that Sochi is a very smart and loyal friend also."

When Sochi heard these words of praise she nearly swooned with delight. She emerged completely from Jasmine's sweater and reached out her little arms to Fleece as if to embrace him. How perceptive he was! How attractive he was! But her arms were too short to reach him and, besides, Jasmine whispered to her to *behave yourself or else*!

Fleece continued with his example: "As I was saying, owning a doll like Sochi is a gift, yes, a priceless gift, a fantastically priceless gift! Now my dear little Miss I want you to think about how you would feel if some sneaky thief came in the night and took Sochi away. Wouldn't you feel terrible?"

"Yes I would," said Jasmine. "So what are you getting at Mr. Fleece?" But before Fleece could answer, Sochi added with great emotion: "She would be inconsolable! She would take ice cold baths! She would cover herself in ashes! She would put pepper in her nose! She would put pebbles in her shoes! She would eat only broccoli and spinach! She would..."

"Please stop your jabbering," said Jasmine to Sochi "and let's listen to what Mr. Fleece has to say!"

Fleece smiled and nodded. "Exactly my point my dear little Miss! You would be inconsolable! But if you had *insurance* you could avoid the terrible tragedy of being left alone without a doll such as Sochi. Yes! If you had *insurance* with us we would replace Sochi with another doll just like Sochi! You wouldn't even know the difference after a while."

Sochi didn't like what she had just heard. She *really* didn't like the idea that she could be replaced so easily. Her feelings for Fleece quickly turned from admiration and attraction to suspicion and hostility. She whispered to Jasmine: "Don't listen to what he has to say. He is ugly and stupid and stinks." In response, Jasmine showed Sochi her impatience by giving her a little shake and shoving her inside her sweater. "So how does this *insurance* work?" she asked Fleece.

"*Insurance* is one of the greatest inventions of all time," said Fleece. "Right up there with the invention of the wheel, the computer, and hot bagels. Here's how it works. Every week you give me a small sum of money, say like $1.25. In return I promise to replace blessed little Sochi here with an exact copy in case she gets stolen or misplaced or runs away. There are a few words you need to remember. For example you become the 'insuree' Sochi is the 'insured object' and I am the 'insurer'. The $1.25 is the 'insurance premium'. So let's say, as an example, that two days after you sign the insurance agreement— and paid your first premium— blessed little Sochi here has a temper tantrum and runs away. Then all you need to do is write a letter to the following address:

Fleece, Flimflam, and 'Stool', Inc.
Professional Insurers
345 Old Lalaville Road
Lalaville, NY 12211

and tell us that you don't have Sochi anymore."

"What should I put in the letter?" asked Jasmine, who had now become quite interested in what Fleece was offering. The $1.25 premium was exactly what Chacha gave her as *discretionary income*—in other words money that she could use in any way she saw fit for, example, to buy a box of Gooeycheweys at the movie house, or to buy Sochi a pair of socks, or to add to her savings for buying a button-making kit.

"It's all very simple my dear, wonderful, blessed little Miss," said Fleece looking at Flimflam and Toadstool with a conspiratorial smile. "I just happened to have a letter written to us by your friend and neighbor Pilata Polonius. If you read it you will see what kind of letter we need to replace the insured object."

Here is what the letter from Pilata said:

April 2, 200X

Dear Messieurs Fleece, Flimflam, and Toadstool:

While I was playing at the house of my first best friend Dorvit, I lost my little red plastic watch, which my mother bought for me at *the flea market in Lalaville for $5. Since I have an insurance policy with you, would you kindly replace my red plastic watch with another. It doesn't have to be red. It could be blue or green.*

Thank you

Pilata Polonius

Jasmine read the letter. She could easily write a letter like that! She began to like this idea of insurance! If she ever lost something that her parents bought for her she could replace it without her parents even knowing that she had lost it. She hated to admit to her parents that she lost something because they would say things like *why don't you pay more attention to where you put things* or *try not to be so scatterbrained* or other things that made her feel bad.

She was ready to make an insurance deal with the Tilops! "All right!" she said, "I think, Mr. Fleece, that I will get insurance for my doll Sochi. I'm so grateful to you for teaching me how important it is to have insurance!"

9. Jasmine topples the Tilops

When Fleece, Flimflam, and Toadstool heard that Jasmine was ready to buy into their insurance scheme they could barely contain their joy. They cackled, whistled, exchanged high-fives, made yuk-yuk sounds, jumped up in the air, did cartwheels, scratched their behinds, picked their noses, and clapped their hands. Finally they calmed down and caught their breaths. "Dear blessed little Jasmine," Flimflam said. "Please give us a minute to draw up the *insurance agreement*. The *insurance agreement*, my lovely little Jasmine, is merely a little document that that spells out the rules of our agreement. The written agreement is sometimes called a *certificate*. The certificate will state that you have an agreement with our company that in the event that unforgettable little Rochi here runs away or is kidnapped, we shall be obliged to replace her to the best of our ability. In return, my priceless, golden little princess, you will pay us the meager, tiny, barely noticeable, trivial, sum of $1.25 per week."

"My name isn't Rochi!" Sochi screamed. "It is Sochi you pickled-headed, smelly little dishtowel. How would you like it if I called you Slimeslam instead of Flimflam?"

But Sochi's voice did not carry very far and Flimflam didn't hear her; after all, dolls typically don't have strong voices. It remained for Jasmine to remind the Tilops that Sochi's correct spelling was S-o-c-h-i.

The three Tilops turned away from Jasmine and went into a huddle. From out of nowhere they pulled out paper, pens, stamps, and other things needed to write a certificate. They worked frantically for a few minutes but in the semi-darkness Jasmine could not see what they were writing. She could hear some sort of murmuring coming from the Tilop huddle such as ...*party of the first part... principal clause...sub-clause...party of the second part... contingency fee...title search...* and so on.

After a few minutes the Tilops were through and the certificate was ready. With great flourish Flimflam stood up as tall as he could get, unrolled the certificate, wiped his brow, and read:

"Hear ye, hear ye, hear ye all!

To all citizens of Lalaville let it be known that on this date, April 18, 2XXX, the honorable firm of Fleece, Flimflam, and 'Stool' have entered into a binding agreement with one

Jasmine Turmalina

to insure her private and personal property, specifically, one doll with the name of

Sochi Turmalina

against kidnapping, and other loss, as defined below in the fine print. Premiums for this outstanding service will begin today and paid, henceforth, weekly to the amount of $1.25. This agreement will be pursuant to the following conditions:

This agreement cannot be transferred. Please note that the insured object is a ragged doll, named Sochi, of poor quality whose worth on the open market is probably less than 75 cents. In addition she seems to suffer from emotional instability, which reduces her value even further, probably to no more than 25 cents. In case she does get lost or stolen the firm of Fleece, Flimflam and 'Stool' (henceforth FF and 'S' Inc) is not obliged to furnish the insuree a doll of value greater than 25 cents. If such a miserable doll cannot be found at garage sales, dustbins, and garbage cans FF and 'S' Inc will pay the insuree the sum of 25 cents or give the insuree one small can of frozen organic turtle food, whichever has the lesser value. If the insuree wishes to cancel this agreement, she must notify FF and 'S' Inc in writing and pay a penalty of $5 or give FF and 'S' Inc her cat Pissoir, whichever has the greater value. This is a legally binding document in full compliance with the highest principles of insurance ethics and fully approved by the Legislature of the State of New York.

Flimflam had not read the small print to Jasmine, claiming that it was too dark to do so. When Jasmine asked him why the print was so small, Fleece said that they, the Tilops, had almost run out of ink and had to write in very small letters. This made sense to Jasmine but not to Sochi. In fact the Tilops had not counted on Sochi's excellent night vision. Sochi had actually emerged from Jasmine's sweater and read the small print while Flimflam was reading with great flourish the main text of the insurance agreement. When she saw herself referred to as 'a ragged doll'... 'a miserable doll'... suffering from 'emotional instability'... having a value of only '25 cents', she felt the greatest hurt of her life. Well maybe not the greatest hurt but the second greatest hurt. The greatest hurt had been when Caesar accidentally sat on her during the whole course of last year's Thanksgiving dinner.

Sochi's hurt turned into a white hot anger. She was ready to explode. Her little arms and legs began to shake and her mouth went dry. But just before she was about to give out the loudest yell anyone had ever heard she remembered something that an aging doll named Sun Tzu had told her, "To yell is easy; to obtain revenge is difficult." She also remembered what the now discarded doll Clausewitz had told her on her third birthday, "Revenge must be served as a cold desert." To Sochi this meant that the best revenge is planned and executed when you are cool, calm, and collected and not when you are so angry that you can't think straight.

So Sochi didn't yell. But she whispered to Jasmine what the small print said. At first Jasmine didn't believe a word of it. But Sochi's voice and her expression convinced her that Sochi was telling the truth. Jasmine became furious and she was just about to call the Tilops, "Liars, Cheats, Hoodwinkers, Virus, Bacteria, Parasites, Slop buckets..." and so on, when Sochi reminded her of what the dolls Sun Tzu and Clausewitz had said. So Jasmine bit her tongue and said nothing.

"Well my precious little princess, are you ready to sign the insurance agreement insuring you against the loss of exquisite little Rachi here?" asked Flimflam. Jasmine looked at Flimflam in wonder; *could he really be that stupid* she thought? "Her name is Sochi, S-o-c-h-i, not Rachi," said Jasmine with annoyance. "Please try to get her name straight," she added. She noticed that Fleece and Toadstool were unhappy with Flimflam for once again getting Sochi's name wrong. They didn't want to upset Jasmine who might decide not to buy the insurance from a group that couldn't even get the name of the *insured object* right. Once again the Tilops went into a huddle and whispered accusations at each other. *Nincompoop... stupid...dimwit...duh... helloooo...bozo brain...Rummi...Wolfi...* were some of the whispers that Jasmine heard coming from the Tilops.

Suddenly Jasmine had an idea. She took out her sardine sandwich and took a bite out of it. The fishy smell of the sardines wafted over the Tilops. The Tilops were not used to the smell of sardines or any other fish for that matter. Living as they did in the back of the shed, the Tilops knew the smells of spider webs, chipmunks, dead bees and flies, decomposing squirrels, fermenting grass from the lawnmower, spilled oil, fertilizer, coal bricks for barbecues, cement and, finally, that of human sweat. But not the smell of fish! Only Toadstool had once smelled something like this long ago but for the life of him he couldn't recall where or when.

"What, my glorious little princess, is that you're eating?" the Tilops asked in unison. They had gotten excited by the smell: it was strange but not unpleasant.

Jasmine was prepared for this question. While the Tilops were sniffing the air trying to make out the odor of the sardines and going sniff, sniff, sniff... Jasmine worked out her plan for getting rid of the Tilops once and for all without hurting them.

"My dear Messieurs Fleece, Flimflam, and Toadstool," she began. "It appears to me that given the business that you, er, gentlemen are in, you are in need of a high degree of smartness to carry out your activities with success. After all not everyone can write these complicated insurance certificates that you gentlemen write. What I have here is the world's finest brain food. It is called *pilchardus juvenus* more commonly known as *sardines*. In your studies in Tilop School you may have learned that the emperor of Russia was called the czar and his wife was called the czarina.

Their children were called *czardines* and in order to become very czmart – I'm sorry I meant to say *smart*—they ate small fish from the Black Sea. These special fish were very expensive and difficult to catch and only the royal family was allowed to eat them. In honor of the royal family the fish were subsequently called *sardines*. It is these very sardines that I have here in my sandwich!"

The Tilops could barely believe what they had just heard. For that matter Sochi could hardly believe it either. "How come you never told me that?" she hissed to Jasmine. "Do I always have to be the last one around here to be told important things?" Jasmine gave her a squeeze to quiet her down.

Fleece was the first to speak. "My dear little dark-haired princess," he said, "surely in gratitude for all we have done for you, you will let us have this magnificent brain food that you call *czardines*—I'm sorry, I meant to say sardines—so that, indeed we can serve the Lalaville public with greater intelligence and scrupulosity. As you see, our poor colleague Flimflam can hardly remember a name as simple as Roochi from one minute to the next and is in bad need of your sardines. I dare say that 'Stool' here—and even I— have shown lapses in memory and judgment, which this magnificent alimentary treasure will surely cure!"

Toadstool frowned at being called 'Stool' but said nothing. He decided that as long as Fleece was going to call him 'Stool' he would call Fleece 'Flea'.

Upon hearing Fleece's words Jasmine at first said nothing. The Tilops became nervous and looked at Jasmine expectantly. Even Sochi became impatient. "They called me 'Roochi'! Are you going to stand there like a statue and do nothing? Or do I have to take matters into my own hands?"

Finally Jasmine spoke to the Tilops. She said, "I will let you have this magnificent brain food but first we must agree to and sign a binding contract. And this contract will state that in return for me giving you these brain-enhancing victuals you will forever leave Lalaville and practice your business elsewhere, perhaps Lutherville or Deltaville. You will also return all the money and items that you took from children in the last thirty days. Whatever money is left over after that you will give to the 'Old People's Fund' so that poor, elderly, people can buy ethnic food such as brisket, tortillas, fried chicken, shrimp-in-lobster sauce, and humus for their religious holidays. This contract will be filed with the Department of Legal Contracts of the State of New York. Please include in the fine print that any violation of this contract will be severely punished. The violator will be used as a washcloth by raw-sewage workers for a period not exceeding thirty days but for at least ten days."

When the Tilops heard this proposal they looked at each other, asked Jasmine for a time-out, and went into a huddle where they got involved in an agitated, secretive, conversation. While she couldn't hear exactly what they were saying she heard words like...*outrageous...unfair...cannot make a living...never accept...no way...*

The conversation went on for a long time. Jasmine became worried; maybe she had pushed her luck too far? Maybe her demands were too outrageous even for the less-than-brilliant Tilops? But then, as she waited for the Tilops to come to some sort of agreement among themselves, she heard a new set of words coming out from the huddle that were very different from the first. She didn't understand these new words but she noticed that the attitude of the Tilops had become less quarrelsome and more agreeable, even optimistic. The new words had a nice ring to them like...*calculus...rocket science...trigonometry...philosophy...linguistics...finite state automata...* and others.

Finally the Tilops emerged from their huddle. They were all smiles. Fleece unrolled a large document, which he called a *binding agreement* and showed it to Jasmine. Jasmine and Sochi read the document with great care. Yes, it promised all the things that Jasmine had asked for and in return asked only for Jasmine to give them the sardine sandwich. The Tilops had already signed the document and now Jasmine did too. Every one shook hands and even Sochi got into the act. She hugged each of three Tilops and even though Fleece said to her *Seeya later Roach,* and 'Stool' had said *Until we meet again Sacha,* and Flimflam had said *Don't be a stranger Sicho,* Sochi had not become angry. She knew that *revenge was being served as a cold desert.*

As the Tilops left the garden and floated out of Lalaville on a burst of wind to make mischief in Deltaville, it finally occurred to Toadstool where he had smelled sardines before: it was at a supermarket where, in the sardine display, one of the cans was leaking. The sardines were on sale for 25 cents a can and could be purchased for next to nothing at any of the thousands of supermarkets in the United States. There had been no need to make a binding agreement with Jasmine! There had been no need to return their stolen goods! There was no need to promise to leave Lalaville and the comfortable shed where they had taken up residence! But all that was behind them. They had signed the agreement and it could not be violated. The Department of Legal Contracts of the State of New York would see to that!

As they floated further and further from Lalaville, they got very upset and began blaming each other for the terrible deal—as they now realized—that they had struck with Jasmine. Passing night birds and bats could hear the Tilops argue: *brain-dead... buffoon... iconoclast...bozo...secularist...pigeon-droppings...purple jelly fish...creepy crawler...*were some of the insults they threw at each other.

Eventually the three Tilops left the puff of wind and transferred to a small low-lying cloud that was aiming right for Deltaville. As they got hungry and shared their sardine sandwich, they became less sad and Fleece said to the others, "I don't know about you guys but I'm getting smarter already!"

"We are too!" said a happy Toadstool and Flimflam.

10. Jasmine enters the maple tree

It was now maybe 4:00 o'clock in the morning. Jasmine and Sochi had been so busy with the Tilops that they had failed to notice that it had gotten very dark. The moon was now hiding behind a cloud and there was an unnatural stillness in the garden. Initially after the Tilops left, Jasmine and Sochi were greatly relieved and happy that they had managed to trick and get rid of the Tilops once and for all. They danced around from pure joy, exchanged high-fives and hugs, and even kisses although Jasmine usually didn't like to kiss her dolls, finding that the moisture from the kisses made them limp. "Yes sir," said Sochi, "I showed those Tilops a thing or two. Why those three poor excuses for handkerchiefs were no match for my brains and bravery! They hadn't counted on my super vision to read the small print! They hadn't counted on my bravery in the face of their threats! They withered when I stood up to them and read them the Declaration of Sochi's Independence! They recoiled when I so fearlessly said 'Give me liberty or give me death'! They trembled when I so beautifully recited 'I regret that I have only one life to give for my friend Jasmine!' I finished them off when I began to sing 'Four score and seven years ago our developers brought forth on this

Jasmine enters the hollow maple

continent, the beautiful suburb of Lalaville, a new development, conceived in profit and...'"

"Excuse me?" interrupted Jasmine. "I don't recall you reading them any 'Declaration of Sochi's Independence' or saying all those other things you claim you said. Still I'm very grateful that you read the fine print. That really saved the day!"

Just as Sochi made ready to rebut Jasmine, the plaintive sound of *Whee-er-yoo* was heard coming from the maple tree. Jasmine and Sochi looked at each other and froze from fear. But Jasmine, being stout of heart, quickly regained her composure and gave Sochi a little hug. "I'll protect you," she said. "After all you are my *first* best friend and I'll let nothing happen to you."

Sochi was not reassured by those words. While she liked being called '*first* best friend', there was not much about Jasmine that inspired confidence: she was only four foot two inches tall and weighed only 70 pounds. She was not a professional wrestler or boxer and didn't know any martial arts like karate and tae kwon do. What chance would she and Sochi have against the Craxies? What horrible monsters lay in wait in the hollow of the maple tree? What beastly things were ready to pounce on them once they were in the hollow?

"Please!" she whimpered. "Let's go back to our warm bed and forget this stupid idea. Let someone else find out what's down that tree. Please, please, Jasmine, let's go back!"

But Jasmine was undeterred. "A promise is a promise," she said. "Now stop your chattering and keep a cool head. I have a feeling that we'll need all our wits about us once we go into the hollow."

They had come to the maple tree. Sochi had taken refuge in Jasmine's sweater and covered her eyes with her small hands. Jasmine stepped into the hollow and was surprised to find a hole there—about the width of a sombrero (a kind of Mexican hat) — leading straight down. She lowered herself into the narrow hole, which was deeper than she had at first thought and not as dark as she expected. There was a dim light at the bottom that enabled her to see what she was doing. Dirt from the sides of the hole stuck to her sweater. At the bottom there was a long horizontal tunnel with smooth curved walls. Jasmine estimated that the tunnel was maybe ten feet below the ground. It was about five feet high and five feet wide and very long: Jasmine could not see the end of it. The tunnel was lit by a dim blue light coming out of the ground. When Jasmine looked more closely she could see that the concrete base that she walked on had a narrow slit from which the light emerged. It reminded Jasmine of the guide lights you see in movie theaters that help you find your seat if you get there late and the main lights have gone out because the picture has started. She couldn't make out the color of the tunnel wall but she guessed that it was gray or off-white. "Mmmm," she thought, "these dull walls could use some decorations, maybe some posters or drawings."

After walking for some fifteen minutes, Jasmine realized that she head heard nothing from Sochi. "Are you O.K in there?" she asked, directing her voice into her sweater. Sochi let out a moan. "I have never been in such a horrible place in my life," she said. "I'm so scared that I can hardly breathe. Please Jasmine let's go back!"

"It's too late to go back," said Jasmine. "When I slid down the hole I realized that without a ladder there was no way to go back up. Since we don't have a ladder we'll have to take our chances down here and go forward!" When Sochi heard this she fainted outright. Jasmine could feel her collapse to the bottom of her sweater. Luckily for Sochi, the sweater fit tightly across Jasmine's waist otherwise she would have fallen out onto the hard concrete floor.

After another ten minutes of walking, Jasmine saw something in the tunnel, maybe about two hundred feet away. The thing seemed to move. When

Jasmine realized that *the thing was actually moving* she got such a shock she thought that her heart would stop!

11. Jasmine encounters Sister Ka

Jasmine's survival instinct prevented her from fainting. She knew that she would have a much better chance to survive the encounter with this...*thing* if she maintained a cool head. After all, by keeping calm she was able to redeem Waxface and defeat the Tilops. So she went forward and came closer and closer to the ...*thing*. "For pity's sake," said the...*thing* in a gruff and angry voice, "I have been calling '*Where are you*?' for hours and hours and only now do you appear!"

So this ...*thing* could actually speak—and speak English no less! This reassured Jasmine since dangerous creatures like wolves, wolverines, and plesiosaurs do not speak English. Because the light in the tunnel was so weak it wasn't until Jasmine was only ten feet away from the ...*thing* that she could see it for what it was: a woman dwarf! The dwarf wore a long black cloak with a hood; the cloak covered the dwarf's entire body. At the waist was a heavy leather belt and in the belt was some sort of flexible stick about three feet long— about the height of the dwarf. The dwarf's hair and neck were covered by the hood and only the face was visible. On the dwarf's nose was a prominent wart with three dark hairs growing out of it. A name tag sewn into the cloak at about the level of the heart identified the dwarf as Sister Ka.

"You are here because you disobeyed your parents!" said the dwarf as she removed her hood to reveal spiky, unkempt hair. "You were supposed to be sleeping in your bed and instead went promenading in your yard in the middle of the night. You risked being attacked by the Craxies and even endangered your doll Sochi! You are clearly a disobedient young girl. Here at BEBE we shall retrain you and teach you obedience!"

So this is where she was, thought Jasmine: *at the Better Behavior Academy for Non-Obedient Girls known as BEBE for short! And this dwarf, this Sister Ka, talking to her in such an angry fashion, must be one of the Monitors that run the place! And the stick in her belt must be the tickle stick she had heard about! Oh Boy!* She thought. *Now I'm in for it. But was it possible that her parents had something to do with this? Would her parents really hand her over to these Monitors for retraining? I mean I'm not a dog am I, that needs to be retrained and go to obedience school? What about the 'Whee-er-yoo' I heard; was that a ruse to get me here?*

While these unpleasant thoughts occupied Jasmine's mind, Sister Ka went on: "Unlike your friends Dorvit and Pilata who listen to their parents, you seem to think that rules don't apply to you. Even your half-brained doll, and 'first best friend', warned you about going out at night and pleaded with you to stay in bed. But no, you wouldn't listen! Well my dear! Now you will have to bear the consequences of your actions!"

Sochi, meanwhile, had recovered from her fainting spell but being stuck in Jasmine's sweater she could not see what was going on. When she heard herself described as "half-brained" she became enraged. "Who in heck's name are you calling half-brained?" she began to say as she poked her head out from Jasmine's sweater. But then when Sochi saw stern-faced Sister Ka with her large nose-wart and the three black hairs sticking out of it, she quickly retreated back into Jasmine's sweater while letting out a moan.

"You will follow me," said Sister Ka. "I will introduce you to the chief Monitor Sister Ze. We call Sister Ze the *Big Sister* because she is our boss. Big Sister is old and wise. She is never wrong! Whatever she says goes! I advise you to treat her with great respect, otherwise you will be sent to your room without breakfast!"

Jasmine followed Sister Ka down the tunnel. She noticed that it had angled down from the moment she had got into it. When she first entered the tunnel it probably was only about ten feet deep. But here, at least a mile from the entry point, the tunnel must have been at least a hundred feet deep—the height of a ten-story building. Jasmine felt like she was going down to the center of the earth. Would anyone ever find her again? Would they miss her at school? Would her parents notice that she was missing? Would Dorvit replace her with another *second best friend*?

Soon they came to a small motorcycle with a side carriage. Sister Ka signaled for Jasmine to get into the carriage and put on the motorcycle helmet that lay on the seat. Sister Ka then put on her helmet, motorcycle goggles, and a pair of heavy gloves. Just before starting the motor, Sister Ka passed a little item to Jasmine. "This is a motorcycle helmet that will fit Sochi. Put it on her and fasten your seat belt!"

Within seconds they were off, traveling down the narrow tunnel at speeds up to 80 miles per hour. Soon Jasmine fell asleep; how long she slept she had no idea.

After many hours they reached the end of the tunnel; on the left was a heavy door that Sister Ka unlocked with a large key that she kept under her cloak. Sister Ka pushed against the door and it creaked open. Jasmine noticed that carved into the door was a phrase in a foreign language:

"Lasciate ogne speranza, voi ch'intrate"

The creaking of the wooden door had stirred Sochi's curiosity. She peaked out from Jasmine's sweater and glanced at the phrase in the door. Her eyes opened wide and she let out a scream. "What is it?" asked Jasmine, truly worried that something had happened to Sochi. But Sochi said nothing. Never had Jasmine seen such a look of horror on Sochi's face. Whatever she had seen must have been the most shocking thing that she ever saw or experienced.

"Listen," said Jasmine. "If we're going to get out of this place someday, I can't afford to have you go into hysterics! Now, tell me: what did you see?"

Jasmine and Sister Ka

Sochi had recovered. "Did you know that I was manufactured in Milan, Italy?" she said. "My original name was Sochia Della Fuego. While I lived in Milan I learned to speak Italian. The sign carved into the door we just passed said...it said... Oh! It is too horrible to translate into English!"

"For the last time what did it say?" demanded an exasperated Jasmine.

Sochi looked at Jasmine with tears in her eyes. "It said...it said...

Abandon all hope, ye who enter here."

When Jasmine heard these words, it took all her energy, her emotions, and her willpower not to break down right then and there. But she knew that now was not the time to lose her head. Besides she had to set an example for Sochi! "Listen," she whispered to Sochi. "Signs and appearances don't mean a thing! Remember how scared we were when we first saw Waxface? And yet by keeping our heads we got the best of him. Same with the Tilops: there were three of them against just the two of us, yet we got the best of them also! I will admit that the sign is scary. But with your, er, intelligence and, er, cunning, and my *sang-froid* we shall overcome!"

"What is *sang-froid*?" asked a tearful Sochi who, despite her tears of fright, was pleased at being described as intelligent and cunning. Jasmine realized that *sang-froid* was a poor choice of words: *sang-froid* is a French idiom that means *to be cool*. But literally translated it means *cold blood*. To use the word 'blood' at a time like this in front of Sochi was not a good idea. So Jasmine simply said, "It means to be cool and brave."

The heavy wooden door closed behind them. Before them was a stairwell that went up to dizzying heights. When Jasmine peeked up the stairwell she could not see its end. "Follow me," said Sister Ka, "and NO TALKING!"

12. The Big Sister

The three of them, Sister Ka, Jasmine, and Sochi began to climb the stairs silently. For Sochi this required no effort since she hung on to Jasmine's sweater. But for Jasmine this was the most amount of work she had ever done. After a while she asked Sister Ka to let them stop and rest on one of the dozens of landings they passed but Sister Ka refused and said that Big Sister was waiting for them. As they climbed the stairwell higher and higher Jasmine began to notice doors leading from the landings at the higher floors. The doors had signs on them like: LAUNDRY ROOM or SILK COLLECTION ROOM or FOOD PANTRY or LIBRARY etc. One of the most bizarre signs was SPIDER RETREAT ROOM. What in the world is a *spider retreat room* wondered Jasmine? Everything was so strange here that Jasmine had the feeling that she had somehow entered an alternate universe totally different from the one she was used to.

Eventually Sister Ka stopped in front of a door marked BIG SISTER'S ROOM. "All right," she said. "This is it. You will be introduced to Big Sister whose name, as you already know, is Sister Ze. You will also meet some of the other Monitors who will want to look you over. Big Sister will tell you about BEBE. You are not to talk unless given permission to do so. Tell your half-wit doll that no backtalk or wisecracks are allowed. If you can't control her, she will be confiscated and placed in the DISCARDED ARTICLES ROOM. This room, which we Monitors call the DAR, is the last stop before the monthly trash removal service comes to remove its contents. So if you want to keep your doll make sure that she behaves!"

Both Jasmine and Sochi trembled when they heard these harsh words. But any struggle at this point would be futile; they were prisoners in this strange place.

Sister Ka took a deep breath and knocked three times at the door. Then she pushed the door open and grabbed Jasmine by the arm and led her to the front of a long wooden table. On each side of the table sat three dwarf Monitors dressed in the same manner as Sister Ka. At the far end of the table sat Sister Ze. Jasmine noticed that all the Monitors had large warts on their noses. Surprisingly each wart had three black hairs growing out of it. The only exception was the wart on Big Sister's nose: it had four hairs growing out of it.

Jasmine looked around the room. It had no windows and the walls were painted a dark gray. There were some drooping tropical plants in cracked ceramic pots in the corners but the plants had long turned brown and were surely dead. There was a painting on each of the four walls showing spiders of different sizes. "These creepy Monitors have something going on with spiders," mused Jasmine. But as yet she had no idea what it was.

"Dear Sisters," said Sister Ka while standing in front of the table. "I want to introduce you to Jasmine Turmalina, a young girl in serious need of behavior modification. She has disobeyed her parents on many occasions. She has ventured into her yard in the middle of the night thereby risking attacks on her and her doll Sochi by the crazy Craxies. She would prefer to play with her friends Dorvit and Pilata than do her homework. She has to be constantly reminded to wash her hands before eating and brush her teeth before going to bed. She..."

"Enough! We have heard enough!" said Big Sister. "It is time to consult with the other Sisters at the table. Do the other Sisters agree that this child needs severe behavior modification?"

The Sisters suddenly began to pound the table with their fists creating a great noise. To Jasmine it sounded like a herd of horses running on a wooden floor. The room shook from fourteen ferocious fists banging on the table.

"Enough!" said Big Sister. "Let the meeting secretary record that the vote was unanimous. Jasmine Turmalina will henceforth be taught how to behave properly. She will be assigned to the Sigma (Silk Generation from Mygalomorphae and Araneomorphae) group and her Monitor will be Sister Do. Will Sister Do please introduce herself!"

The dwarf Monitor named Sister Do stood up. In a gravely low voice she said, "My name is Sister Do, Do as in *dou*ghnut," and then sat down. "Very good! Very good, indeed," said Big Sister. "Now I ask the other sisters who will be in charge of Jasmine's progress to introduce themselves!"

Next a Monitor whose name tag said Sister Re stood up. "My name is Sister Re," she said. "Re as in sting*ray*." Big Sister looked pleased." "Superb! Truly superb," she exclaimed.

What was so 'superb! Truly superb' about standing up and giving your name? thought Jasmine.

"My name is Sister Mi, Mi as in *mi*dget," said the next monitor. Jasmine saw that Sister Mi had a kind face and that when she said *midget* a tear rolled down her cheek. "Excellent! Most excellent," said Big Sister. "Continue please!"

A monitor on the other side of the table stood up. "My name is Sister Fa," she said, "Fa as in *fa*tigue." "Well done! Well done indeed," said Big Sister. "Next?"

The Monitor sitting next to Sister Fa stood up. Jasmine saw that she wore glasses and seemed nervous. "My name is Sister Sol, Sol as in *sol*dier," she said. "Brilliant!" said Big Sister.

Jasmine was puzzled: what was so 'brilliant' about saying that your name was 'Sol, as in soldier'? She began to wonder if Big Sister wasn't a little cracked like the forlorn pots in the corners. She predicted that the next Monitor's name was going to be Sister La. Sure enough, at the urging of Big Sister, the sixth and last Monitor stood up and said, "My name is Sister La, La as in *La*gomorph."

This statement was greeted by absolute and uncomfortable silence. Jasmine, who expected Big Sister to say something like "Fantastic!" or "Magnificent", was surprised at the silence. But the silence didn't last long. Big Sister stared at all the monitors and finally returned her gaze to Sister La. "Pray tell dear Sister La, what in the world is a Lagomorph?" she asked.

Sister La looked embarrassed and looked down at her lap. Then she pulled out a carrot from beneath her cloak, put the carrot in her mouth and began to chew it. When this happened some of the Monitors began to pound the desk. "Silence!" said Big Sister. "I do believe that Sister La is playing a game of charade with us! She is trying to tell us what a Lagomorph is by giving us clues! Anyone who thinks she has the answer is free to take a guess!"

"It is a turtle," said Sister Do.
"It is a donkey," said Sister Re.
"It is the angel of the carrots," said Sister Mi.
"It is a laptop computer," said Sister Fa.
"It is a carrot-eating flatfish," said Sister Sol.
"It is a flamingo," said Big Sister.

"It is none of the above," giggled Sister La. "If Big Sister will allow me, I can provide another clue. It appears that such a clue might be useful."

All the Sisters agreed that another clue was needed. Sister La took out two handkerchiefs and rolled them into two soft tubes. She then stuck the tubes into her ears and made them stand-up straight. The overall effect was of a creature that ate carrots and had long ears.

"It is a crocodile," said Sister Do.
"It is a mule," said Sister Re.
"It is the angel of the corn," said Sister Mi.
"It is a laptop computer," said Sister Fa.
"It is a carrot-eating goldfish," said Sister Sol.

"It is a goldfinch," said Big Sister.

Sister La could not control her giggling. Finally she said, "It is none of the above. With your permission I would like to give you one more clue. Is it all right with you Big Sister if I give all of you one more clue?" Big Sister agreed but the game was getting out-of-hand. It was clear that the Sisters were getting annoyed that they could not guess what a Lagomorph was. It made them feel stupid. They began to grumble.

Suddenly Sister La jumped up on the table and got on all fours. She raised her behind and quivered her nose. Somehow she had gotten another handkerchief, which she had fashioned into a white tail, and attached it to her rear end with a safety pin. She hopped back and forth on the table all the while eating the carrot.

"It is an alligator," said Sister Do.
"It is a rhinoceros," said Sister Re.
"It is the angel of the quadrupeds," said Sister Mi.
"It is a laptop computer," said Sister Fa.
"It is a carrot-eating catfish," said Sister Sol.
"It is a pelican," said Big Sister.

"It is an *Oryctolagus cuniculus*, the common #@&%* rabbit!" screamed Sochi who had emerged from her paralyzing fear. What is it with you people? Have you microscopic brains? I mean does an alligator eat carrots? Does a laptop computer have long ears? Does a catfish walk around on all fours? Give me a break!!"

Jasmine realized that Sochi's outburst was going to get her into deep trouble. The room had become so quiet that you could hear a feather drop. Whispering out of the side of her mouth, Sister Ka said to Jasmine, "I told you to control her. What happens to her now is not my doing!"

Big Sister looked at each of the Monitors and they looked back at her. Then, as if responding to some silent signal, they all began to pound the table. The noise was thunderous– Jasmine thought that her eardrums would break. Sochi, knowing that the worst was yet to come retreated into Jasmine's sweater, moaned, and passed-out.

The table-pounding stopped as quickly as it started. "Sister Ka: Take this offensive doll and put her in the DAR," said Big Sister. "And as for you Jasmine, if you do not surrender Sochi peaceably and you force us to take her from you, we will mail her by FedEx ™ to the Craxies, for them to do with as they wish. It is your choice!"

Shocked as she was, Jasmine knew that she had to keep a cool head. Giving up Sochi without a fight was against her nature and made her feel disloyal to Sochi. But she knew that if it came to a fight she would easily be overpowered by the monitors, resulting in Sochi being mailed out to the Craxies who were known to be cruel and pitiless. On the other hand if she gave up Sochi peaceably, Sochi would be put in the DAR where it would be several weeks before the trash removal truck came to take her away. During that time all kinds of things might happen. Jasmine might figure out a way to save Sochi or Sochi might figure out a way to save herself. Big Sister might even have a change of heart and reunite Sochi with Jasmine. Also some of the Monitors might take a liking to Jasmine and help her get Sochi back. In particular Jasmine saw that Sister Mi believed in angels and how bad can a person be who believes in angels? Taking all of this into consideration Jasmine decided to hand over the unconscious Sochi to Sister Ka. As she did so, she saw a look of pity on the face of Sister Mi. Jasmine figured that in a truly desperate situation Sister Mi was the most likely Monitor to help her.

As Sister Ka left the room holding the unconscious Sochi, Jasmine had another thought: no matter how many clues that Sister La gave to the Sisters, Sister Fa always gave the same dumb answer 'a laptop computer'. To Jasmine this meant that whatever plan she hatched to escape from this miserable place, it was Sister Fa who could be most easily tricked.

13. The Story of BEBE

"Since you will be a guest of BEBE you are entitled to know how BEBE came to be and how it is run," said Big Sister. "Please sit down," Big Sister continued, "Sister Mi will bring you some water. We know that you are tired and confused and unhappy that Sochi was taken from you. Life will not be easy for you here but if you do the work to which you've been assigned and follow our rules you will, one day—in the far future—, be released from here."

Big Sister continued: "Perhaps you are too young too be aware of this but all over the world there are rich, happy, families whose children are beautiful and bright. The parents of these children take them for horse-back riding lessons, music lessons, ballet lessons, drawing lessons, and what have you. When the child happens to be a girl there are so-called coming-out parties for her so that she can make her social debut to *society*. These parties are called *debutante balls*. Are you following me so far Jasmine?"

Jasmine was listening carefully for a clue to where this speech was heading. At the same time Sochi's absence left her brokenhearted. She promised herself that come-what-may she was going to save Sochi. "Yes, I have heard every word that you said, Big Sister," she said.

"Good," said Big Sister, "I shall go on. These young debutantes wear beautiful, expensive dresses, and have cosmetic experts that help them look beautiful by applying make-up. When they are all dressed up, make-up and all, these young women are among the most beautiful living things on this planet. Their families show them off as if they were precious jewels, which in a sense they are. They are *even more* precious than precious jewelry!"

Big Sister spoke with increasing passion. "These young women go to the finest private schools and get tutors to help them get into the most desirable colleges. Once they are in college they grow into beautiful marriageable young women. In college they often meet handsome and wealthy young suitors and choose the ones they want to spend their lives with. When their studies are over, they marry and have beautiful and talented children and the cycle repeats."

Big Sister stopped to take a drink of water; Jasmine did too. Suddenly Big Sister asked Jasmine an unexpected question. "Did your parents ever take you to a fancy restaurant?" she asked. "Yes they did, once. I think that they were celebrating their anniversary and couldn't find a baby-sitter for me," answered a puzzled Jasmine. "Right," said Big Sister, "and I bet the place was beautiful, the table setting spectacular, the service attentive, and the food outstanding. Am I right?"

Jasmine tried to remember the event. Unbeknownst to her parents she had taken Sochi with her and Sochi had been telling her silly gossip about Hypolux and Optimus during the dinner. Thus Jasmine didn't really pay much attention to her surroundings. Still she said to Big Sister: "It was nice."

"But you probably didn't wonder about what happens in the kitchen, did you?" asked Big Sister. "In the kitchen is where all the not-so-nice things happen. Fish are degutted, meat is hacked, chickens are dressed and all the left-over food and the remains from the food preparation are thrown into garbage cans. Then the garbage cans are put out into the alley when they start to smell too much. The stink from the garbage cans attract rats that carry disease, etc. Believe me it's much nicer to be in the restaurant than in the kitchen or the alley. Yet without the kitchen and the means to dispose of all the smelly stuff, the restaurant couldn't exist! Do you agree?"

Jasmine had never thought about such things. Moreover, she couldn't figure out what all this talk about restaurants and kitchens and garbage cans and smelly alleys had to do with the story of BEBE. "I guess so," said Jasmine rather timidly.

Big Sister continued her narrative. "You see Jasmine the world is not a perfect place. There is beauty, yes, but there is ugliness also. You might even say that without the ugliness there can be no beauty!"

Jasmine didn't know whether to agree or disagree. These were all new ideas for her and she hadn't had the time to think about them. She decided to remain silent.

"Yes, beauty needs ugliness as the farmer's beautiful green crops need the ugly brown and smelly fertilizer," continued Big Sister. "And that's where we, the Monitors, come in. We are the uglies that enable the beautiful to exist. Without us there would be no beautiful people in the world. We are like sponges that soak up the malformed, the ugly, the warts, the too-short, the not-so-smart, the obese, the too-thin, those with long noses and crooked teeth, the hunchbacks and all the other deformed creatures that nature has chosen to plague. Of course in the new global economy everybody has a specialization and we at BEBE have our own: we absorb the plagues of shortness and warts. You, dear Jasmine, will grow tall because we shall absorb the shortness that threatens you. You will have blemish-free skin because we uglies will attract the warts meant for you!"

"This building, the one we are in right now, was built for us by a German architect named Miscast Pander Woe who was a leader of the Badhouse School of architecture. It is full of hallways that lead nowhere, rooms inside other rooms, fake ceilings, windows that open onto brick walls, doors that never open, other doors that never close, secret passages that lead to dark tunnels that lead to underground lakes, and rooms without doors or windows that can never be entered or exited. In other words, Jasmine, there is no escape!"

For a moment Jasmine thought that Big Sister was finished but this was not the case. "Our funds—that is to say the money we need to run the place—comes to us from Mr. George Tsouris , whose wife, Fecund, delivered three identical triplet girls who proceeded to be extremely unruly. He searched high and low for a place where they could learn good behavior. But other than dog-training schools he could find nothing. So he started this place and called it BEBE. His three daughters were the first graduates of BEBE and went on to become famous people. You may have heard of them: they go by the professional names of Golda Meier, Margaret Thatcher, and Hillary Clinton."

Jasmine had not heard of these women. But that didn't mean anything because Jasmine almost never went to the movies and she didn't know one actress from another. "Anyway my dear," said Big Sister, "you now know enough about BEBE to satisfy your curiosity. Sister Do will be your Monitor and will follow your progress. The Sigma Brigade, to which you've been assigned, does very important work. Only our most difficult students get assigned to the Sigma Brigade. But in time, Jasmine, when your behavior improves, you will be given easier work. But now it's time for you to get enrolled!"

At this point Big Sister turned her face away from Jasmine and said to the other Sisters: "Let the meeting secretary record that the 11,533rd meeting of the Sisters' Council is now over." The news that the meeting was over led the Sisters to pound the table with great vigor for one full minute. The noise was so loud that Jasmine had to put her fingers in her ears.

Sister Do and Jasmine left the room by the back door and walked down a short hallway to another door. On the door was a sign that said

Enrollment Office

Sister Do opened the door with a long, hooked, key. Inside the room there was a large brown desk with an empty flower pot on it and many empty coffee cups. Behind the desk sat one of the Monitors. Her name tag identified her as Sister No and she wore thick glasses. On the left side of the desk stood an old desktop computer; a small metal tag riveted onto the computer said **Property of BEBE Inc**. *So this is it*, thought Jasmine, *this is where I become an official resident of* BEBE.

14. Jasmine is enrolled at BEBE

Sister Do led Jasmine to the front of the desk and quietly left the room. Without looking up at Jasmine Sister No said: "So you claim to be Jasmine Turmalina. Do you have any identification to prove it? For example a driver's license, credit cards, social security card, bank card, etc?"

Jasmine thought hard. She didn't have any of those things and didn't even know what some of them were. What in the world was a bank card or a social security card? She wasn't even sure what a credit card was but she once heard her mother Chacha tell Caesar that she bought a beautiful hat decorated with fake fruit like bananas, grapes, and pineapples with her *credit card* because she didn't have enough cash. So a credit card must be something that you use when you don't have any money. But in that case why didn't people stop going to work to earn money and use credit cards instead?

"I'm just a kid," said Jasmine. "I don't have any of those things. At home I have a report card with my name on it. It has mostly B's on it but I got an A+ in gym and in Creative Play. If you let me go home, I'll get my report card and prove to you that I'm Jasmine Turmalina."

"Very clever, very clever indeed!" chortled Sister No. "You are trying to trick me into letting you go home to get your report card. But once I let you go you would not come back!" *Oh yes I would!* thought Jasmine. *I would come back with Caesar and Chacha and the police, if necessary, to rescue Sochi. Maybe even bring the Army!*

For the first time Sister No looked up. "Yes, I can see that you are Jasmine Turmalina," she said. "After you sign your admission form, Sister Do will take you to the Costumerie where the Costumer will fit you with an approved BEBE outfit. These outfits are designed to remind the wearer that BEBE is not an amusement park or play station. You will be allowed to keep your jeans, tee-shirt, and sweater. After that you will be taken to the Sigma

Office where they will give you the tools to do your job. Now do you have any question?"

"Yes, I do," said Jasmine. "Is a Costumer the same as a Customer?"
"No," said Sister No. "A Costumer has the o before the u, while a Customer has the u before the o."

"That's not what I meant," said Jasmine. "I mean, like, could a Costumer be a Customer? Could a Customer be a Costumer?"

"Yes and no," said Sister No. A Costumer could be a Customer if he or she has the money and seeks to buy something. A Customer could be a Costumer if he or she has the talent and went to Costumerie School."

"Well, what do you actually learn in Costumerie School?" asked a thoroughly confused Jasmine. *Obviously she wasn't getting through to Sister No*, she thought.

"In Costumerie School, you learn how to be a well-informed Costumer," said Sister No. "But I think that we have exhausted this subject," she added. "Next you will want me to explain Cosmogony or Cosmography, or even Cosmology. Do you have any other questions?"

Jasmine had many questions. But she had trouble communicating with Sister No. She would restrict herself to only the most basic questions regarding her stay at BEBE.

"Will I have my own room?" asked Jasmine.
"No," said Sister No.

"Is there a TV at BEBE? I like to watch my favorite show, The Adventures of the Corpulent Manatees." asked Jasmine.

"No," said Sister No.

"Will I ever get to see Sochi again, my doll and first best friend?" asked Jasmine with some anxiety.

Sister No turned to her computer and got her browser to access Google™. Jasmine saw her type in *Will Jasmine Turmalina get to see Sochi?* But she couldn't see the response. Then Sister No typed in some more stuff. Finally she hit the log-off button and turned to Jasmine. "I don't know, "she said.

Sister No's answer was better than getting a flat No, thought Jasmine. *So there was hope that she would get to see Sochi after all!*

Sister No gave Jasmine the enrollment form to sign. The enrollment form said:

Hear Ye! Hear Ye! Hear Ye!

To all of sound mind and lacking the will, spirit, or means to engage in criminal activity:

Let it be known that henceforth the enrollee

Jasmine Turmalina

has been duly enrolled in the Better Behavior Academy for Non-Obedient Girls (BEBE) where she will undergo rigorous training in the art(s) of good behavior and polite conversation.

_____
Signature of enrollee

_____
Signature of enroller

As soon as the enrollment form was signed Sister Do appeared, as if by magic, to take Jasmine away. Sister Do could not have come in through the same door that she and Jasmine had entered because that door was large and heavy and creaked when it opened or closed. So Sister Do must have come through some other opening in the room. Jasmine looked around but the only opening that she saw was an air vent in the corner of the room. Had Sister Do crawled into the room through an air vent? It was possible since none of the Sisters were more than three feet tall and were pretty narrow across the shoulders. This was good information to know when Jasmine got around to planning her escape.

"Are we done here?" asked Sister Do. For no apparent reason Sister No crushed one of the empty coffee containers and began to pound the desk with her free hand. Apparently Sister Do made her tense. "Yes," Sister No said. "She's all yours now." And with that she took out a piece of smelly cheese from her desk and began to chew it as if she hadn't eaten in days.

Sister Do and Jasmine left the room. The next stop was the Costumerie. Jasmine was surprised and pleased to find another girl her own age there. One of the Costumers was fitting the girl for an official BEBE outfit. Jasmine wanted to speak to her but a large sign hanging on the wall gave the following warning:

NO SPEAKING UNLESS SOMEONE SPEAKS TO YOU FIRST

To Jasmine the sign made no sense. Since no one could be the first to speak according to this rule, there could never be any conversation. For example if she spoke to the girl first she would be in violation of the rule; but if the girl spoke to her first then the girl would be in violation of the rule. Maybe, Jasmine figured, the rule didn't apply to the Sisters. But then the sign should have said:

NO SPEAKING UNLESS SOMEONE SPEAKS TO YOU FIRST
(This does not apply to the Sisters)

The girl was given a dark blue, loose-fitting pair of pants and a dark gray sweatshirt with long sleeves. Her name tag said *Cortina* and the back of her sweatshirt said **Property of BEBE** and underneath that it said **Sigma Squad.** The Costumer gave Cortina a baseball cap and told her to keep it on when she was doing her job *otherwise you will get spider eggs in your hair*! "What kind of job will I get that might give me spider eggs in my hair?" asked Cortina. "Your job will be described to you in the Sigma Orientation Office," said the Costumer. Then a Monitor by the name of Sister Ta led Cortina out of the Costumerie.

"Next!" bellowed the Costumer. Jasmine was next but she didn't understand why the Costumer had to yell "Next." After all she stood only about three feet away. The Costumer measured Jasmine's height and bellowed "Forty nine inches!" and almost immediately another Costumer came with a brown parcel and guided Jasmine to a changing room where she put on her new outfit. It was identical to Cortina's except her name tag said *Jasmine*. When she came out of the changing room she was given a black baseball cap. "Wear this cap when you are doing your job," said the Costumer, "otherwise you will get spider eggs in your hair!"

Jasmine knew well enough not to ask why she might get spider eggs in her hair. She knew that she would have to wait until she got to the Sigma Orientation Office. She hoped that she would get to see Cortina there. Without Sochi and her friends Dorvit and Pilata she was beginning to feel very lonely.

Sister Do, who had been sitting quietly and reading a copy of *The Great Outdoors* magazine while waiting for the Costumer to finish, suddenly stood up and said, "It's time to go the Orientation Office. That's were you will be told about your job." She led Jasmine out of the Costumerie and back into the hallway. Soon they stopped at a door marked

SIGMA ORIENTATION OFFICE

"O.K," Sister Do said. "I will bring you inside and leave you. It is very important that you pay attention to what the teacher, Sister Wa, says. Sister Wa is a world renown scholar on spiders. She has written many scholarly articles and books on spiders. Her specialty is *Theraphosa leblondi*, the world's largest spider, found only in remote parts of northeast South America. Sister Wa is a household name in many countries because of her exciting discovery that *Theraphosa leblondi* can be distinguished from each other by an intricate pattern of dots on their fangs. In Fetidstan and other central Asian countries, they celebrate Sister Wa Day by exchanging spider eggs. Please treat Sister Wa with great respect because we want Sister Wa to be happy here. There are rumors that several top universities would like to hire her. I've been told that one university has offered her ten million dollars to start a nano-arachnida research laboratory. Nano-spider science has a very promising future; for example people are training spiders to enter the gullet of people who are chocking on something, like a piece of steak, and maneuver the obstruction out of the way. Spiders can be trained to go into your ear canal and remove the wax build-up. But most important of all it seems that it may be possible to get spiders to go inside the body to check out if everything is OK. For example if you have a tummy ache you swallow a board-certified *Araneus quadratus* and it goes down into your tummy and checks everything out. Pretty neat, eh?"

To Jasmine this wasn't neat at all. The idea of having spiders running around her ears or in her tummy did not turn her on. But she didn't say anything and let Sister Do bring her into the room.

15. Jasmine learns about spiders

The Sigma Orientation Office wasn't really an office at all. It was much more like a classroom with a number of tables and four chairs at each table. There were several girls sitting at the various tables and Jasmine recognized Cortina. She went to Cortina's table and sat next to her. Sister Wa stood on the podium and waved to Sister Do, who waved back and quickly left the room. On a large desk standing on the podium stood a giant model of *Lycosa scutulata*, more commonly known as the wolf spider. Hanging from a roller on the front wall was a canvas picture of a gigantic spider showing all the important parts of its skeleton, digestive system, and reproductive organs. The different parts were identified by complicated words: *anterior cephalothorax, prosona, opisthosoma, chelicerae* and others. The whole thing turned Jasmine off; in fact had she not been sitting next to Cortina she might have freaked out.

"Ahem," said Sister Wa holding a long pointer and pointing to the spider on the canvas, "what we have here is the female black widow spider, so called because she often eats her male partner. Note the swollen posterior abdomen; this one must have just finished having her mate for the main course. The first pair of appendages, the *chelicerae*, hide a pair of fangs that secrete a particularly nasty poison; not a good idea girls, to keep these little creatures as pets!"

Sister Wa continued: "The next pair of appendages, the so-called pedipalps, serve as feelers. In the male the pedipalps contain a reproductive organ. Then there are four pairs of legs making a total of eight legs. But the most interesting thing is that at the rear of the spider's abdomen are a pair of modified appendages called spinnerets that are used to secrete silk. This silk is much stronger than steel and is used for making insect traps called spider webs. Once an insect is caught in a spider web, the spider wraps it in more silk and paralyzes it with a bite from its fangs. Spiders are so smart that if you move them in a zero-gravity environment such as in a spacecraft, they will adapt to the environment and still spin an effective web. I'd like to see one of you do that ha-ha!"

Sister Wa looked around to see if everyone was listening. Satisfied that everyone was, Sister Wa continued: "Here at BEBE, the Sigma squad collects the spider-webs created from the suborder *Labidognatha*. The silk is used to make shoes for the Sisters who have very delicate feet. Spider silk is extremely soft and durable; one pair of shoes made from spider silk can last a lifetime. Are there any questions?"

An African-American girl by the name of Sibasi raised her hand. "Just how we supposed to get them webs?" she asked.

"An excellent question," answered Sister Wa. "You will be given a special tool called a web-collector. The web-collector was invented by German engineers working for the American Army in 1946. When the web collector is placed near the web, it attracts the web to it like a magnet attracts metal filings. As the web is drawn to the web-collector you slowly spin the web-collector until you amass a large spool of silk. Then another tool called the spool-remover will remove the spool. The spool of silk will then be put into a special box called a spool-collector. When the spool collector is full you will bring it to a closet called the Texas spool repository."

Next, an Italian girl by the name of Tossa de Mar raised her hand: "How many hours a day do we have to work?" she asked.

"A superb question," answered Sister Wa. "You will wake at five am in the morning and be fed breakfast. Your workday begins at six am. You will work until noon and then be fed lunch. At two in the afternoon you will return to work and work until four. Then your workday will be over. From four to five you can rest or sleep or play calm games like checkers or chess or the new game *Catch the fleas!*, the latest import from China. At five you will promptly shower, brush your teeth, take your vitamin pills, polish your shoes, comb your hair, and dress for dinner. Dinner is from 5:30 to 6:30 pm. From 6:30 to 7:30 you will receive instructions in obedience. At 7:30 pm you will prepare for bed. By eight, you will be in your beds and the lights will go out. Any more questions?"

A Ukrainian girl, named Chernobylia, asked: "Will the spiders bite us? How do we make it impossible for the spiders to go into our noses and ears?"

Sister Wa smiled. "An unusually astute question my dear," she said. "First of all, the spiders are sleepy at six o'clock in the morning from spinning their webs all night long. Then you shall be wearing special web-collecting gloves made by the BiteNoMore™ Company that are spider-bite proof. You will also wear caps that will prevent the spiders from laying eggs in your hair. Finally, spiders don't usually like to go into people's noses or ears. In the fifty or so years that BEBE has been in existence there has been only one case of a spider going into a girl's nose. The girl suffered no ill affects but we knew that something was wrong when we found her chewing on a springtail (*Collembola Orchesella*) a kind of wingless insect. The problem was easily solved by putting some pepper in her nose and causing her to sneeze. The spider was shot out of her nose with the force of a cannon blast. I'll take one more question and then the orientation session will be over."

A French girl named Framboise was called on. She spoke with a heavy French accent. Jasmine wondered what she was in for.

"I have ze question," said Framboise. "Zees *araignée*, I mean spiders, zay must leev somewhere non? If we take away zeir *toile*, I mean zeir webs, zay have no place to leev, non?"

"A brilliant question, yes, truly brilliant," said Sister Wa. "You have addressed a moral issue of great concern. The spiders are disoriented only for the brief period after we remove their webs. Then they start to rebuild their homes almost immediately. Are the spiders homeless while they are rebuilding their webs? Certainly not! When you are *building* a home or actually own one you are not homeless! We can take an example from those brave folks that live in south Florida, around Homestead. Every time the wind blows, or it rains, their homes fly away or dissolve into mud. Are those people ever called homeless? Certainly not! They contract with builders who bring lots of cardboard and rebuild their homes. These folks are not homeless: they are urban pioneers! The same with our spiders: they are urban arachnids!"

Sister Wa looked around triumphantly to see if her point had been absorbed. Framboise seemed confused but didn't say a word.

"Besides," Sister Wa said, "after every ten thousand inches of silk weaving our spiders spend a whole week in the SPIDER RETREAT ROOM where they are fed the most delicious imported rare insects by 80,000 servants and 72 dark-eyed, adoring, *Pholcus phalangioides* (daddy longlegs). It is sometimes tough to coax the spiders to get back to work spinning webs after such a vacation but they know what awaits them after they finish the next ten thousand inches of silk."

Jasmine couldn't follow the logic of Sister Wa's argument. As Jasmine reasoned, you either had a home or you didn't. Just because you might be building a home didn't mean that you couldn't be homeless.

Jasmine noticed that in BEBE the Monitors often used such words as 'brilliant' or 'astute' or 'excellent' or 'superb' when answering questions. She recalled that Big Sister said things like 'well-done' and 'truly superb' and 'most excellent' and brilliant' when the Sisters were introducing themselves in that very first meeting. This must all be part of her *obedience and polite conversation training* she figured. The Monitors were setting an example that they expected the students to follow when they left BEBE; Jasmine liked the idea of talking in this exaggerated polite manner. She could imagine her mother asking, "How was your day dear?" and Jasmine answering, "An astute question Mom, most astute!" or Caesar saying, "I worked really hard today," and Jasmine saying, "Well done Dad, very well done!" Her parents would be proud of her and maybe Dorvit would make her her *first* best friend if she talked that way around Dorvit. Dorvit might say, "My piano teacher likes the way I play Mr. Chopin's *Ètudes*," and Jasmine might say, "An excellent observation on your teacher's part my dear, most excellent!" How grown-up it sounded! Jasmine had once seen a movie that took place in a haunted mansion in a country called England. The butler in the haunted mansion spoke the same way. Maybe people would think that she was English if she talked that way. What fun!

16. Jasmine goes to her room

After all the enrollment business and the Sigma orientation was completed, there had been barely enough time for dinner. The little girls were brought into a large room that had several long tables. There were four such tables with sixteen seats on a side. Jasmine had calculated that there was enough room for 128 misbehaving young girls to eat at the same time. Jasmine looked for Cortina and was happy to have found an empty seat next to her. When Cortina saw Jasmine she smiled; while, as yet, the two girls had not talked to each other much, they had formed a silent solidarity pact. There was a good chance that one day they might become friends.

Sisters Do, Re, Mi, and Fa were ladling out the food from four large tureens that each stood on a food cart that rolled on four little squeaky wheels. Jasmine got a ladleful of tomato puree with white kidney beans. It looked awful but Jasmine was hungry and began to eat some anyway. Surprisingly, it wasn't as bad as it looked and before long Jasmine had eaten her whole portion. She had looked forward to desert but when it came and she looked at it she had to turn her head away. Calf's foot jelly is not pretty to look at: it quivers when you touch it and there are little pieces of bone and meat suspended in a semi-transparent, gray, gluey gelatinous mess that looks like Jell-O™ gone bad. At home she would never have eaten it, telling her mother, "Not an excellent choice for desert, Mommy dearest. Definitely not a most excellent choice!" But at BEBE things were different. Here and there she could hear one of the girls laughing hysterically, no doubt a victim of the feared tickle sticks. The Sisters enforced discipline and all the rules of BEBE by using tickle sticks. The Sisters carried the tickle sticks under their arms and when, say, a girl refused to eat, the Sister would touch the girl with the tickle stick and the girl would laugh uncontrollably for a good two minutes. After such an experience the girl would have even eaten frozen frog- legs if told to do so.

Because Jasmine was not in a laughing mood and therefore wanted to avoid the tickle- stick, she ate the calf's-foot jelly. It was greasy and smelly but it didn't taste too bad. Besides, Jasmine had learned in school that meat and bone, in any form, contained lots of protein and protein is what made you strong. And Jasmine was going to need all the strength she could get if she

---

Reader: A Greek goat herder named Dimitri, who wanted his goats to learn good behavior, is given credit for inventing tickle sticks. Dimitri's goats were known to be the most poorly behaved goats in all of Greece. Dimitri's goats were so spoiled that they refused to eat hay or grass and would only eat imported Italian spaghetti flavored with extra-virgin olive oil. Any other goat herder would have lost patience with such animals and would have turned them into goat cheese. But Dimitri loved his goats—especially one called Beatrice—and wanted them to learn good behavior without causing them pain. So one night, after drinking a kind of Greek Cool-Aid™ called Ouzo, Dimitri invented the tickle stick.

---

was going to save Sochi and escape.

Since she was a newcomer to BEBE, Jasmine was allowed to skip the 6:30 to 7:30 evening obedience session. Sister Do escorted Jasmine to the room that would be hers for the duration of her stay at BEBE. To reach the room, they had to walk up six flights of stairs in a narrow windowless stairwell that led to a large room—the so-called East Wing—that connected the main part of BEBE to another structure called the East Tower. There they took an elevator a long way up until they got to Jasmine's room. The room had six bunks, three on each side of a pair of opposite walls. All four walls were painted a different color. The bunks were arranged vertically—one on top of the other—and Jasmine was assigned the lowest bunk on the wall painted purple. In the middle of the room was a wooden table with six chairs, three on each side. Along the wall painted green stood a large wardrobe closet—called an armoire— where Jasmine and the other girls sharing the room could store their belongings. The third wall—painted yellow—contained a sink with hot and cold running water and a small mirror mounted above the sink. The last wall—painted blue—contained the other three bunks. Next to the door was a list containing the names of the room's occupants. Jasmine was pleased to see that Cortina was on the list; the other occupants were Framboise, Chernobylia, Sibasi, and Tossa de Mar. The room had no windows but a second door opened onto a balcony from which Jasmine could see the surrounding countryside. The room was very high up, maybe 300 feet above the grounds below. Jasmine could make out that BEBE was housed in a castle-like structure with four high towers. Her room was in the East Tower; there was no chance to escape by way of the balcony. When Jasmine looked southeast she saw a vast green forest. Beyond the forest were thousands of little lights. To the north was an arid and broken landscape from which ugly billows of yellowish smoke arose from holes in the ground and ugly vulture-like things flew around in circles. Far, far to the northwest Jasmine could make out a vast, black lake.

The BEBE castle

In all her life Jasmine had never seen such an unreal landscape. Not even when she went to visit Aunt Yalte who lived in a place called the Bronx!

"Ahem," said Sister Do. "I suggest that you put your things away and get to bed as soon as possible. Tomorrow will be a long day and you will need all the rest you can get. In the armoire you will find pajamas, a hairbrush and comb, and all the things needed for good personal hygiene. The bathroom is next to this room and at night there will be a light in the floor that will guide you to the bathroom if you need to use it. The armoire also stores some books and games, like checkers, chess, dominos, and *Catch the fleas!* When you play *Catch the fleas!* you are responsible for putting all the fleas back into the flea box that comes with the game."

Jasmine had no intention of playing a game called *Catch the fleas!* She found the name of the game repulsive and couldn't image anyone playing such a stupid game even if it did come from China. Suddenly she found herself very sleepy and yawned. "You'll be asleep in 30 seconds," said Sister Do. "I will leave you now and wish you goodnight." And with that Sister Do left the room and quietly closed the door.

Within seconds Jasmine had changed into her pajamas, brushed her teeth, and used the bathroom. "Tomorrow is another day," she said to herself just before jumping into her bunk. She was asleep within five seconds.

17. Jasmine collects spider webs

Jasmine found herself stuck in a large spider's web. How she got there she had no idea. When she freed one hand the other hand would get stuck. If she freed one leg the other leg would get stuck. She knew that she was in trouble and that the more she wiggled the more likely that the spider would come out of its lair and attack her. But she couldn't stay in the nest forever because that would make the Monitors angry. So she tried even harder to pull away but without any luck. Then it happened: a large *Tegenaria gigantea* (also known as a house spider) came out of its nest. Its simple eye scanned the web and very soon discovered Jasmine. "My feast has begun," the spider said, "I smell the blood of an Englishmun!" It came closer and showed its fangs. Jasmine began to scream: "But I'm not English! I'm just a little girl from Lalaville. I don't deserve this! Please, please, don't bite me!"

But the spider didn't hear her and came closer still. Just as it began to touch her with its first pair of walking legs a tremendously loud DING-DONG was struck. Jasmine fell out of the web and landed in her bed!

She had been dreaming! But the sound of the bell going DING-DONG was real. She was startled and disoriented but when she saw the other girls leaving their bunks to go wash and dress she felt better. There *was no spider* and she *wasn't stuck* in a spider's web! Cortina smiled at her and said, "Good Morning Jasmine. You had better hurry because the Monitors will be waiting for us in the dining hall with breakfast prepared." Framboise gave her a brush and said, "Zees *brosse*—I mean brush—is for your *cheveu*—I mean your hair. The other *brosse*, ze one in the *armoire*, is for your chausseurs—I mean ze shoes. Do not get zees brosses mixed up because ze one for ze shoes steenks like ze feesh!"

It wasn't easy to understand Framboise but Jasmine got the message: one brush was for brushing her hair and the other was for polishing her shoes and the shoe brush, for some reason, smelled like fish.

After washing, dressing, and combing her hair, Jasmine joined the other girls on their way to the dining hall. This meant walking down six long flights of stairs on an empty stomach. It occurred to Jasmine that this might be the way that the Monitors got the girls hungry enough so that they wouldn't complain when fed potato sandwiches.

The Sigma squad had its own table in the dining hall. Several bottles of warm milk stood on the table. Some potato sandwiches were wrapped in brown paper while others were wrapped in green paper. Jasmine asked Sibasi what the colored wrappings meant and Sibasi answered that the green-wrapped sandwiches were for girls with green skin while the brown-wrapped sandwiches for brown-skinned girls. "Naw," Sibasi said, "I'm only kidding! The green wrapped sandwiches are low-fat while the brown-wrapped sandwiches are salt-free." Sibasi smiled at her. "You see," Sibasi added, "these sandwiches are made by elderly and retired Monitors who live in a retirement community called Midgets Manor in Florida. They are very concerned with things like salt and fat. They say that too much fat clogs the arteries and too much salt raises your blood pressure."

Jasmine took a bite out of her green-wrapped sandwich: it tasted like wet cardboard. She began to really regret that she ever went out into the yard in the middle of the night against her parents' orders. Never had she eaten food this bad. Tears came to her eyes.

"Zees foot steenks," said Framboise. "It is worsed than ze rotten Camembert."

"How I miss my Ukrainian breakfast of pickles, herring, yogurt, and beets," said Chernobylia. "These potato sandwiches are not even fit for plant food."

"The worst pizza in all of Italy is better than this *spazzatura*, this *rifiuty*, *this immondizia*," said Tossa de Mar.

"Even old *haggis* is better than these potato sandwiches," said Cortina who spoke with a Scottish accent.

"Good Lord," said Sibasi. "Cold chitterlings dipped in ketchup taste better than this stuff."

Jasmine didn't understand many of these words. She had never heard of Camembert, chitterlings, or *haggis*, or any of the strange words that Tossa de Mar used. But it was clear to her that she was expected to say how bad the food was by comparing it to something truly awful. So she said, "These sandwiches are worse than broccoli."

The other girls agreed. They gave Jasmine approving nods.

Soon a bell rang DING-DONG; it meant that breakfast was over and that the girls had to return to their rooms to change into their work clothes. For the Sigma squad the change in clothes didn't amount to much: the girls merely had to put-on an apron, a baseball cap, and a pair of BiteNoMore™ gloves. For other squads the work clothes were more elaborate; one squad had to put-on scuba gear and another squad had to put on clown suits. Jasmine was intrigued by these outfits and wondered what kind of work required such weird outfits. Sister Do took the Sigma squad to a large elevator and pushed the button that took them to the attic of the BEBE castle. When the elevator door opened the Sigma girls immediately knew that there were spiders around. The smell of dust, spider silk, mildew, and egg sacks reminded them of the fetid smells they encountered in the basements of their homes, especially near the ground-level small casement windows that had never been opened or in the basement's moist dark corners where layers of cobwebs shared space with hundreds of spider egg-sacks.

Each of the girls picked up an assignment card from a small table that gave them the location of the webs that they had to collect. Jasmine's card said

A6 R1-R36

Sister Do explained that Jasmine's assignment, until further notice, was to collect all the webs in rows 1 to 36 (R1-R36) in aisle six (A6). Jasmine was given a web collector and a spool remover, put on her hat and BiteNoMore™ gloves and went to work. Pretty soon she found aisle six and applied her web-collector to the web in R1. It worked like magic! As soon as the web collector came near a web it attracted the silk to it and when you rotated the web-collector slowly, a spool would begin to form much like thread on a spindle.

The sleepy spider at R1 came out of its nest to see what was happening. When it saw that its web was being rolled-up it bared its fangs and wiggled its pedipalps. But it was so sleepy that it crawled back to its nest and went back to sleep. After about 10 minutes, Jasmine had collected her first web. "Wow! That was easy," she said to herself. "If I can do all the webs in 10 minutes each then I'll have worked only six hours and I'll have two hours off." But such was not the case. Some of the webs were quite large and required fifteen minutes to collect. Moreover, the web-collector sometimes stalled and Jasmine had to shake it in the same way that her mother shook a thermometer when she wanted to get the mercury down.

By the time she finished R7, Jasmine realized that her web-collector had a thick spool on it. It was time to apply the spool remover. The spool remover fit over the web-collector shaft the way the cap of a pen fits over the nib. Then when you squeezed the spool remover and slowly pulled it out, it dragged the silk off the shaft of the web-collector and Voila! The spool of silk was gone and the web-collector was ready for re-use.

The web at R9 was small and untidy as if the resident spider didn't care. Jasmine was considering whether this web was even worth collecting when the resident spider came out. This surprised Jasmine because she had not disturbed the web. She could see its simple eyes and the unkempt hair on its body. For some strange reason, Jasmine had the feeling that this was no ordinary spider.

"So they sent a new one to hassle me and force me to rebuild my web every night," the spider said in a grumpy voice. "Well you get what you pay for! You want my web? Well take the crummy thing! See if I care! And since I am a spider, beware my fangs: the Sisters shall grant me justice!"

As a rule Jasmine didn't care for spiders. To tell the truth she was slightly frightened by them. Ordinarily she would have ignored this spider, even if it could speak! But rescuing Sochi and getting out of this weird place was her top priority. Maybe this strange creature could help her.

"My name is Jasmine Turmalina," she said. "I have been assigned to collect your web. I'm really sorry but the Monitors are forcing me to do this. I have nothing against spiders even though they are, er, funny looking. In fact we learned in science class that spiders are beneficial, er, creatures. They eat mosquitoes and flies and other unpleasant insects."

"I like your style, honey," said the spider. "My name Arie Schnid and I'd shake pedipalps with you but seeing how you don't have any we'll just have to skip the touchy-feely stuff."

Jasmine felt sorry for this wretched, unkempt -looking spider. She tried to make nice by saying, "Please forgive me for taking your web Mr. Schnid. I hope that it will not cause you too much pain."

"Forgive you? Forgive you for my pain?" cried Schnid. "Would you take the fur from a cat, the tail of the dog, the whiskers of the ferret? Has not a spider an eye? Has not a spider pedipalps, *chelicera,* feelers, passions, appetites? Are we not fed with the same food, hurt by the same predators, suffer the same wounds, healed by the same means, warmed and cooled by the same summer and winter as other carnivores? If you step on us do we not squash? If you tickle us do we not agitate? If you poison us do we not die like common insects? And if you take away our webs, shall we not seek revenge?"

Jasmine didn't completely understand this little speech but she liked its rhythm. She now realized that collecting webs without a spider's permission was an issue of great importance to Schnid and decided then and there that she would never take away his web. While Schnid couldn't see her very clearly he could make out the look of sympathy and empathy on Jasmine's face. His words had turned her from an unwilling enemy into a friend.

"Listen, little lady," Schnid said. "I know that you've got a lot of silk to collect so I won't keep you. But if you ever need a favor you can count on me! Oh! And call me Arie, OK?"

"Until tomorrow Arie," Jasmine said. "I'm very glad that we have become friends."

The rest of the morning passed uneventfully. The web collector and the spool remover devices did most of the work. Most of the spiders were too sleepy to offer much resistance. Here and there a spider would try to heave its egg sac onto Jasmine's hair but the baseball cap that she wore caused the sac to roll harmlessly to the floor. Pretty soon the spool-collector box was full and Jasmine brought it to the Texas spool depository. Jasmine didn't quite understand why the storage closet was called the Texas spool depository. Was she in Texas? For the first time since she got to BEBE Jasmine realized that she didn't know where she was. The thought depressed her.

At exactly noon the bell rang DING-DONG. The Sigma girls removed their gloves, aprons, and hats and met Sister Do at the elevator. The elevator took them to the dining hall and the Sigma squad went to sit at their own table.

Glasses of warm pear juice were distributed around the table. Sister Do ladled out oxtail soup to each of the girls. "Eat," she ordered. "This soup is made from the tails of the finest oxen. Oxtail soup is a delicacy and available only in the best restaurants around the world. Do not feel sorry for the oxen. They are meant by nature to lose their tails; this is what they were put on earth for. Those of you who had the good luck of growing up in gourmet households will also appreciate the pear juice. It is the famous Chapeau Shtreimel 1993 vintage."

"Zis foolish woman does not know of what she speaks," whispered Framboise. "She means to say zat the pear juice is a *Chateau* Shtreimel 1993. *Chapeau* wiz ze <u>pee</u> means ze <u>hat</u> in French. Chateau with ze <u>tee</u> is ze <u>castle</u> where ze wines, liquors, and juices are made."

Unfortunately for Framboise, Sister Do's hearing was very good. We tend to think that because people are handicapped, such as the dwarf Sisters were, that their senses are not sharp. Sister Do took out her tickle stick, frowned, and came dangerously close to Framboise. "No my dear," she said. "Zis foolish woman does know of what she speaks," she mimicked. *"And I do mean Chapeau Shtreimel* 1993 *vintage.* The pears are crushed in these fur-brimmed hats called *Shtreimels* worn by people called *Zaddiks.* The nectar from the pears filters through the hat and is collected in bottles for sale at upscale supermarkets. This particular vintage was filtered in 1993!"

Eventually Sister Do and the other Monitors went to eat lunch at their own table at the other end of the dining hall. Every now and then Jasmine could hear the Monitors pound the table with their fists. They liked playing the game charade and Jasmine guessed that the pounding was a form of applause whenever someone guessed the word or phrase. At Jasmine's table it was now possible to talk about serious things like how to escape from BEBE without being overheard by one of the Monitors.

"It is not posseeble to *échapper*, I mean to do ze escape from zees place," said Framboise. "We do not know where ze rums go. If we go into ze wrong rum zen we are in beeg trouble!"

Jasmine guessed that Framboise was saying that without a map of the BEBE castle there was no way to find the right room leading to an exit. Moreover if you got trapped somewhere you faced severe punishment from the Monitors. "We need help from one of the Monitors," said Cortina. "Maybe one of them will feel sorry for us and lead us out of here. Some of them have kind faces. But suppose you go to the wrong Monitor and ask for help and she reports you to Big Sister. Then on top of the obedience session they make you go to *the re-education session* led by *Sister* Re. I heard that's no picnic!"

"Tell me about it baby!" said Sibasi. "I been to them *re-education sessions* several times and them Monitors sure enough knows how to give you a hard time. Sister Re makes you write 'I will be good' five thousand times on the blackboard. Then you'se got to do them *yoga exercises* to 'rid your body of escapist feelings'. Then all the while you do them yoga things, they play this record where one of the Monitors—I think it's Sister Fa— with a guitar moans '♩ I shall not escape/ BEBE is my fate/Big Sister is my guide/ Big Sister's on my side. Oooh, Oooh, Oooh,...♩' And then they play that stupid song over and over while you'se doing the yoga thing. It's enough to give you cramps!"

Tossa de Mar looked as if she would faint. "I would rather drink the water in the canals of Vénezia then go to this *spazzatura* re-education session. Even Mussolini didn't torture the partisans the way the Monitors torture us!"

"To me the greatest torture is not to have my Ukrainian breakfast of pickles, herring, yogurt, and beets," said Chernobylia, "although the yoga thing sounds pretty awful."

As usual, Jasmine didn't quite understand many of the things that were being said. She had never heard of Yoga, the canals of Vénezia, *spazzatura*, and Mussolini. The word *partisan* she could understand: these were people who went to parties a lot. But why this annoyed this guy Mussolini so much that he wanted to torture them was beyond her.

Jasmine thought of Sister Mi; she had a kind face and was the most likely Monitor to help her escape. Also if any of the Monitors was likely to be tricked it was Sister Fa. Jasmine had picked-up on the fact that Sister Fa had little in the way of brains. But to escape BEBE Jasmine needed a plan and she didn't have one. She needed help. But who among the inhabitants of BEBE could provide such help? Who would lead her and Sochi and maybe the other girls out of this crazy place? It had to be someone who knew the place from top to bottom; someone who was brave and reliable. Where would she find such a person?

Meanwhile the girls started telling each other what had brought them to BEBE. Chernobylia was the first to speak. "In the Ukraine, herring is a very popular food. But it is expensive because we import it from Norway. The local herring is not good to eat because it makes you glow in the dark. When people eat the local herring their teeth and hair fall out and their feet begin to smell. Also at night no one wants to be with these people because they give off so much light that you can't sleep. So when my little brother Donetsk was three years old my parents bought him a jar of herring from Norway as a birthday present. When they were not looking I took some of the herring from his jar for myself and I replaced it with the local herring. That night he began to glow in the dark and my parents found out what I did. As a punishment they sent me here. My little brother doesn't glow anymore but one ear has become larger than the other. My parents say that it is because he ate the local herring that I gave him."

When Chernobylia finished her story, all the girls pounded the table with their fists. It was a habit they picked up from watching the Sisters. Not wanting to be the exception, Jasmine pounded the table too. It bruised her knuckles.

Framboise spoke next: "In Paree, zei have zis leettle boats that go up and down the rivière—I mean rivair—called ze Seine. When my mozair had her anniversaire, oops I mean ze birzday, my fadair took us on ze boat. On ze boat I got into a zpitting contest with my friend Adrènal to see who could crasher, I mean zpit the longest into the rivair. When ze wind blew ze zpit ze ozer way, it landed on my fadair's new silk cravate, oops I mean ze tie. My fadair did not like zis too much and, as I had done zis before, he send me here."

As best as Jasmine could make out, Framboise's father took them on a boat ride in Paris to celebrate her mother's birthday. On the boat Framboise and Adrènal got into a spitting contest to see who could spit the furthest. The wind caught some of the saliva and redirected it onto her father's silk tie. The angry father sent Framboise to BEBE.

When Framboise was finished with her story, the girls pounded the table in appreciation. It was now Cortina's turn. "Last Christmas we went to visit my Uncle Harry in Dundee, Scotland where he keeps horses on his farm. Uncle Harry had trouble sleeping because of a toothache and his horse Ragweed had trouble poopin' because he ate too many oats. So they sent me to the local drugstore to pick up some sleep medicine for Uncle Harry and laxative pills for Ragweed. The pills looked pretty much the same. On the way back I met some girls and we raced to see who could run the fastest. Some of the pills spilled out of my pocket so I put them back not knowing which was which 'cause I didn't want to tell my parents or Uncle Harry that I stopped to play instead of coming right home. Pretty soon Ragweed slept all the time and Uncle Harry was poopin' and tootin' all the time. My parents figured out what happened and sent me here to learn 'obedience and responsibility'."

Cortina's story provoked a lot of laughter and fist pounding. All heads now turned to Tossa de Mar. "In Rome we live in a big house on the Via Aurèlia where we keep two dogs called Romulus and Remus. I love these dogs and would do anything for them. One afternoon when everyone was out of the house I decided to make a little party for me and the dogs. Inside the refrigerator I found lots of good food including meatballs, fresh steaks, shrimp, patè, pasta, lasagna and a wonderful cake made with fruit and fresh cream. What a party it was! The dogs were sick for two days afterwards. But my parents were very unhappy with me because all this food was supposed to be for a dinner party that my parents were making for my father's boss, Nero, and his wife Rhea Silvia. When my father did not get his promotion at the Dolce Vita candy company where he worked he decided it was my fault and sent me here. How was I supposed to know that all this food was for the boss and his wife?"

Tossa de Mar's story was very sad. Framboise looked as if she was going to cry. "How injuste—I mean unfair—ze life is!" she cried. Nevertheless the girls pounded the table with extra vigor in appreciation of Tossa de Mar's story.

It was now Sibasi's turn. "I live in Chicago where they got those elevated trains that takes you all over the place. Them trains is called the El and they got like different colors for different trains routes, like, the Green Line takes you south, the Blue Line takes you west, the Red Line takes you north etc. There is this one line, called the Orange Line that takes you to Midway Airport. One day my aunt Kanisha and I were going to Midway to fly to Detroit to visit my other aunt Nakisha. My aunt Kanisha told me not to eat on the train because it was forbidden by the transit police. When she was sleeping, I took out my two-pound bag of popcorn and started eating it. At the Randolph and Wabash stop, where they got that big store Marshall Field—now they call it Macy's— thousands of them pigeons flew into the train car to try to eat my popcorn. Those darn pigeons stayed in the car eating the popcorn until the stop at Midway where they got off when they heard that Midway was the last stop and all passengers, including passenger pigeons had to get off. There was so many of them pigeons that they had to close Midway Airport because them pigeons 'posed a risk to the aircrafts'. Did I ask them pigeons to get on the train to eat my popcorn? My aunts Kanisha, Nakisha, and my mother Mykishka decided that I needed *behavioral modification.* So here I am!"

"How tragique!" said Framboise. "How unfair!" said Tossa de Mar! "How not-cricket!" said Cortina. "How revolting!" said Chernobylia. "What a weird story!" said Jasmine. The familiar fist-pounding followed the end of Sibasi's story.

Finally it was Jasmine's turn. Jasmine didn't know how much to say. She figured that she would tell a highly abbreviated story of her adventures and if the girls wanted to know more she would tell them. So she began with how her friends Optimus and Hypolux told her about the noise coming out of the hollow maple at night and how she had promised them that she would look into it by going out at night against her parents' instructions. And once she was in the hollow maple there was no going back and how the Monitor Sister Ka led her to BEBE.

But Jasmine's abbreviated story didn't satisfy the other girls; they wanted to know more. So Jasmine told them about her and Sochi's adventures with Waxface and the Tilops and how she helped the former and tricked the latter. And when the girls had heard the whole of Jasmine's story they realized that here was a natural born leader: a girl with an original mind and a fearless— well almost fearless—disposition. If they were ever going to escape from BEBE, Jasmine would be the one who would find a way.

The fist pounding that followed Jasmine's story was subdued, almost as if the girls didn't want to bring the Monitors' attention to the fact that here, right under their noses, might be the liberator, the Moses that would lead the girls out of bondage into freedom and the Promised Land—their homes!

At exactly two o'clock the bell went DING-DONG and the girls were led back to their rooms to change once more into their work clothes. Then Sister Do led them back to the attic where they resumed their work. Jasmine had already collected all the webs from R1 to R30 during the morning period so she had only six more webs to collect. So she took her time. As she collected the webs she tried to get to know the spiders better. The spider in R34 was a big guy with large fangs and long hairy legs. He tried to bite Jasmine through her BiteNoMore™ gloves but all he got were little pieces of plastic fibers in his fangs. Jasmine felt sorry for him. Unlike the other spiders who were mostly asleep or groggy from sleep, he was agitated. *Surely he suffered from a sleep disorder*, thought Jasmine. Jasmine recalled that her father Caesar once told Chacha that he hadn't been able to sleep and Chacha got him some medicine called Benadryl. If Jasmine could find some Benadryl she would give him some. None of the spiders except for Arie Schnid could or would speak. But the little spider in R36 had a little sign hanging from his web that said:

> Please do not disturb. I don't disturb you when you sleep do I?

So Jasmine was extra careful in collecting his web. She must have been successful because the spider never stirred.

The four o'clock DING-DONG told the girls that their workday was over. The girls removed their working gear and waited for one of the Monitors to come and get them. Pretty soon the door was unlocked by Sister Do. After a brief inspection, Sister Do approved the girls' efforts and led them back to their room.

For that day, at least, there was to be no more spider-web collection!

18. Jasmine attends an obedience session

Back in their room the girls relaxed. Framboise took out a book in French called "Les Petites Filles modèles" ("The Well-behaved Little Girls") by someone called La Comtesse de Ségur. Her father Henri had given it to her and told her to memorize the whole book. Cortina took out a small orange colored book called "Geeta for Children" by someone called Swami Chinmayananda. It was all about how the Indian God Krishna teaches his disciple Arjuna the "Supreme Knowledge". *Do you like reading this stuff?* Jasmine had asked. Cortina replied that it was very difficult to follow but that her parents thought that an exposure to Indian religion would make her less frisky and more thoughtful. Maybe her stay at BEBE would teach her some *supreme knowledge* of good behavior.

Tossa de Mar lay on her bunk and soon fell asleep. *Roma, Ombrone, Citavécchia, Firenze, Urbino* were some of the words that she murmured while she slept. Jasmine had no idea what these words meant. She knew that Tossa de Mar was homesick for Italy so maybe these were names of Italian places.

Chernobylia and Sibasi decided to play *Catch the fleas!* They took out a wooden box from the closet and put it on the table. Inside the wooden box was a stopwatch, another little box and a spoon-like device for catching fleas. The spoon-like device looked like a spoon with top that could be lifted by pressing a little trigger on the spoon handle. If you pressed the trigger the top would open; if you released it the top would close thereby trapping anything inside. It reminded Jasmine of a utensil that her mother had for storing the proper amount of tea leaves for making a single cup. The stopwatch had two buttons on it. If you pushed one button the stopwatch would start counting time. If you pushed the other button the stopwatch would stop counting.

The little wooden box contained 12 jumping fleas. They couldn't escape because the top of the box had a little removable screen. Once the screen was removed the fleas immediately jumped out and the stopwatch was turned on. The idea was to catch the fleas and put them back into the screened box in the least amount of time. The game could be played by any number of people; the winner was the person who caught all the fleas in the least amount of time.

Fleas are normally very, very small and therefore hard to see much less catch. But Chinese scientists had mastered the principles of *nano-technology* and managed to attach to the tiny fleas even tinier lights called *lasers*. These powerful lights were attached to the flea's back through a process called *electron-beam lithography*. With these lights on their back the fleas could be seen even in total darkness. As they jumped around seeking freedom, the fleas looked like tiny stars moving in a black void.

Reader: *Catch the fleas!* can be purchased* on the Internet for three easy payments of $19.95; shipping and handling is an extra $46.95.*Scylla and Charybdis Imports assumes no responsibility for the state of the fleas upon arrival. All sales are final. No C.O.D's. Only one sale per customer unless you order more. Flea maintenance contract: one year is $113.95; two years $572.67. We recommend Scylla and Charybdis authentic, organic, flea food obtained from licensed blood banks. One year's supply available for three easy payments of $16.96; shipping and handling is an extra $46.95.

Sibasi went first. She was very dexterous and caught all the fleas in one minute and 33 seconds. *Surely* thought Jasmine *there was no way that Chernobylia was going to beat that.* But Jasmine hadn't counted on Chernobylia's experience with catching and killing fleas. Back in the Ukraine, Chernobylia slept on a mattress given to her as a present by her uncle Zhytomyr for her ninth birthday. What Zhytomyr didn't tell Chernobylia was that he had bought the mattress used and had sprayed it with some French perfume to make it smell like new. Zhytomyr had bought the mattress from a Greek goat herder named Dimitri (Yes reader! The same Dimitri of the tickle sticks!) and it was infested with fleas. From her ninth birthday on, until she was sent to BEBE, Chernobylia hunted and killed the fleas in her mattress. She had become so good at it that some of her neighbors paid her small sums to kill the fleas in their mattresses.

Chernobylia caught all the fleas in 59 seconds. She was strongly tempted to kill them but resisted this urge knowing that they were the key pieces in the game.

At five o'clock pm the girls put away their books and games and went to clean up. Jasmine was a little shy about showering with the other girls so she waited until they were done. She brushed her teeth, combed her hair, cleaned her nails, and took her vitamin pills. Then she brushed her shoes and dressed for dinner. Soon Sister Do came to collect them for the trip to the dining hall. Once again the meal consisted of tomato puree with white kidney beans and calf's foot jelly.

The Sigma girls were quiet during dinner. Except for Jasmine, they were thinking of the obedience class that would follow dinner. Jasmine was thinking of Sochi and escape; she missed Sochi greatly and while these girls were nice their company could not fill the void left by Sochi's absence. She promised herself that she would spend more time planning an escape than wasting time such as watching the silly *Catch the fleas!* game.

Just before 6:30 the familiar sound DING-DONG told the girls that dinner was over and it was time to attend obedience class. There were several obedience classes and the Sigma girls and others were assigned the class taught by Sister Wa. The obedience classroom was very similar to an ordinary classroom except that dead or dying plants sat in clay pots along the walls. A large picture of Big Sister hung on the wall at the front. A single 40-Watt bare bulb hanging from an electric cord furnished all the light in the room. Sister Wa sat at her desk in front, under the picture of Big Sister, sternly gazing over the class. The expression on Big Sister's face was one of disapproval as if to say *I never saw such badly behaved girls*. There were about twenty girls in the class; Sisters Fa and Re were the Monitors assigned to act as the *promotion of virtue and prevention of insolence police*; both were armed with tickle sticks. They wore white armbands with the red letters PVPIP on them. Jasmine guessed correctly that these were the initials of *promotion of virtue and prevention of insolence police*.

"Ahem," said Sister Wa. "Since we have a number of new people in the class, I need to find out how bad the current disobedience problem is. The best way to do this is to give all of you a simple multiple choice test. You will have thirty minutes to complete the test. Will Sisters Fa and Re distribute the test please?"

Soon the tests were distributed. Jasmine saw that there were ten multiple-choice questions. They were quite difficult:

1. You are in the movie theatre and you are bored by the film. Then you: a) throw your popcorn at other viewers; b) claim that you have to go to the bathroom but spend your time in the theatre lobby playing video games; c) sit quietly until the movie is over; d) make a noisy fuss until your parents drag `you from the theatre.

2. Your younger sibling (brother or sister) has gotten more ice cream for desert than you. Then you: a) have a temper tantrum; b) eat your portion without complaint; c) trade your dish with the sibling's when no one is looking; d) trick your sibling into giving you his/her portion.

3. Your best friend got a brand new bike. Then: a) you tell her what a beautiful bike it is; b) you tell her that your bike is much better; c) pester your parents to get you a new bike; d) tell her that she was adopted.

4. Your parents invite Aunt Clara over. Aunt Clara hugs you too tightly and pinches your cheek. Then: a) you say "Aunt Clara, I hate you!" b) you step on Aunt Clara's toes; c) you hide when Aunt Clara comes; d) you appreciate that Aunt Clara loves you so much.

5. You find out that your friend has spread rumors about you. Then: a) you spread even worse rumors about her; b) you challenge her to a mudfight; c) you meet with

her to find out why she is spreading rumors about you; d) you lodge a formal complaint with her parents.

6. Your mother just had your best dress cleaned but despite her warnings you climb a tree and rip and dirty the dress. Then: a) you tell your mother the truth about what happened; b) you blame the family pet; c) you try to fix the tear using needle and thread and rub-off the dirt using a steel wool pad; d) you claim that you have no idea how it happened.

7. Your mother has prepared some nice vegetables including spinach and broccoli for dinner. Then: a) you claim to have a stomach ache and can't eat; b) you spill your plate on the ground and argue that you can't eat 'dirty food' c) you make believe that you eat the vegetables but when no one is looking you spit it out into a napkin; d) you eat the vegetables without complaint.

8. Aunt Clara buys you three pairs of brown socks for your birthday and you are disappointed. Then: a) you thank Aunt Clara for the gift and keep the socks; b) you say "Aunt Clara, I hate you!" c) you exchange the socks for your friend's crayons; d) you let the dog or cat chew on the socks.

9. In trying to trace out your favorite drawing, your younger sibling accidentally destroys it. Then: a) you hide your sibling's favorite toy; b) you patiently show your sibling how to trace a drawing without destroying it; c) you tell him/her that he/she is adopted; d) you tell your parents that your younger sibling did it on purpose.

10. Your mother has saved a slice of ice-cream birthday cake for your Aunt Clara. Overcome by hunger and desire you eat the cake. Then: a) you tell your mother that the dog or cat ate it; b) you admit that you ate the cake and say you're sorry; c) you admit that you ate the cake because you had a stomach ache and you thought that eating the cake would soothe it; d) you claim to have no idea as to what happened to the cake.

Jasmine thought long and hard about the answers. Finally she came up with 1-b; 2-c; 3-c; 4-c; 5-a; 6-c; 7-a; 8-c; 9-d; 10-c. She handed in the answers expecting a good grade. She was surprised to see that she got a zero. Sister Wa had written on her paper that she, Jasmine, was in bad need 'moral re-education'. The correct answers were 1-c; 2-b; 3-a; 4-d; 5-c; 6-a; 7-d; 8-a; 9-b; 10-b.

"Your general performance on this exam," said Sister Wa to Jasmine, "and the nature of your answers indicate that you have a passive-aggressive, game-theoretic mindset in which you try to minimize the penalty function instead of maximizing the reward function. Moreover you seek a local minimum instead of a global minimum and that is what gets you into trouble!"

Jasmine had absolutely no idea what Sister Wa was talking about. Was she even speaking English? Sister Wa saw the puzzled expression on Jasmine's face. "In other words," she said with a slight smile, "every time there is a problem or you feel thwarted you look for some tricky scheme to avoid the pain that the situation is causing you instead of dealing with the problem in a straightforward and honest manner."

Jasmine was still confused by this explanation but less so. As she understood it she, Jasmine, used tricks to get out of situations she didn't like rather than try to resolve the situation once and for all. "For example," said Sister Wa, "take your answer to Question 6. Rather than having to face your mother's discontent, you think that by fixing the dress on your own and cleaning it with steel wool it will hide the fact that you went tree climbing against your mother's wishes. But she'll find out anyway because you don't know how to sew well enough to repair the tear and if you clean the dress with steel wool you will destroy it. So in the end you won't have a nice dress and your mother will be doubly mad at you!"

Jasmine realized that Sister Wa made good sense. Sister Wa's explanation was like a light going off in Jasmine's brain! How she wished she could take the test again!

In this way Sister Wa went over the test results for each girl. "Sibasi," she said, "you did rather well but your answers reveal an unrestricted, extroverted, personality with signs of manic aggression. For example in Question 5 you picked answer (b). What good would it do to get into a mudfight with your friend? Other than getting really dirty, would it solve anything? It would be much better to talk to your friend and find out why she is spreading these rumors about you."

"I tell you what good it do," said Sibasi with some heat. "When I done with her she gonna think twice before she tell them lies about me!"

Sister Wa next turned to Framboise. "In your choices I detect a mixture of Russian nihilism and excessive French rationalism," she said. For example take your answer to Question 3. You picked choice (d) figuring that by telling your friend that she was adopted she would get so depressed that she would lose interest in her new bike and you would be free to ride it all you want. That is quite rational. But by discounting the effect of such a lie on the emotions of your best friend you have rejected the optimistic moral principles of Western Civilization and exhibited an almost pure nihilism!"

Jasmine had no idea what Sister Wa was talking about. But apparently Framboise did because she said: "But zis is how we French zink! Zis is why we are the greatest *pays*, Oops, I mean ze greatest country in ze world!"

And so it went. Pretty soon the hour was up and the girls were allowed to return to their rooms under the guidance of Sister Do. On the way out of the classroom, Jasmine saw a small first-aid box hanging on the wall; when no one was looking she looked inside the first-aid box and saw a small bottle of Benadryl. She shook the bottle and one pill came out. That would last the insomniac spider years. She looked forward to giving it to him.

When the Sigma girls got back to their room they quickly washed their faces, brushed their teeth and got into their pajama. They were so tired that they were all asleep even before the lights went out. All except Jasmine that is: she lay awake thinking about what Sister Wa had said to her. Sister Wa had gotten it right: Jasmine was always looking for a trick to get out of facing a problem. A vast mental curtain had opened up before her and Jasmine understood for the first time in her life why she was in trouble so often. This new understanding of her behavior made Jasmine a much stronger person.

But there was one other thing that kept Jasmine awake: she had to find and free Sochi and escape from this place. Nothing was going to get in her way!

19. Jasmine gets help

The next day was pretty much the same as the day before. After breakfast the Sigma girls went to collect spider webs in the attic. Jasmine went to aisle six but before she even started she went to the web at R34 and left the Benadryl pill there. The big spider came out of its nest, fangs showing, sniffed the pill and took a tiny bite out of it. Almost immediately it became drowsy and could barely make its way back to its nest before falling sound asleep. Jasmine was glad that she had found a cure for the spider's sleep disorder.

Nothing eventful happened until Jasmine came to R9. "Good morning Arie," said Jasmine. "Remember me?"

"Do I remember you?" said Arie. "Of course I do!

> *Shall I compare thee to a summer's day?*
> *Thou art more lovely and more temperate;*
> *Rough winds do shake the darling buds of May;*
> *But thy eternal summer shall not fade."*

Jasmine didn't completely understand this greeting but she felt that she had been complimented. She liked the way that Arie talked; it reminded her of the way her teacher Miss Acapela sang the Star Spangled Banner—with feeling and rhythm.

"Listen kid," said Arie in a half-whisper, "word is getting around to the brother and sister spiders about your behavior. You had better be careful!"

"What did I do?" cried Jasmine. "You know I've been ordered by the Monitors to collect the webs! There's not much I can do about that. But I've tried to be as nice as possible to the spiders, poor things. What more can I do?"

"You misunderstood me," said Arie. "The brother and sister spiders, who are my friends, know that you got sleep medication for Taurus in R34 and how you gently removed the web from Atrax in R36 so as to not wake him. Atrax is a light sleeper and he really appreciated it. And finally they know that you didn't take away my web because of my depressed state. I've been depressed for a long time. My therapist says it has to do with an unconscious fear of hornets. In time, she says, I'll get better. Right now she is using behavior modification therapy (BMT). In BMT she makes these fake paper hornets and lets them sit on me. First one, then two, then three, until I start to wiggle my spinnerets from panic. It's really scary but she keeps reminding me that they're only paper hornets. My fear of hornets started when I was barely more than an egg and my father threatened to feed me to hornet larvae when I misbehaved."

"Anyway," continued Arie, "you've shown that you are a true friend of spiders and the brothers and sisters are prepared to help you escape. When I warned you to be careful I meant that from now on you've got to be extra careful around the Monitors. If they find out what you're up to you will never get out of here!"

Jasmine was astounded. The fact that Arie and his brother and sister spiders were going to help her get out of BEBE was the best news she had heard in a long time. She felt like jumping in the air and yelling Yes! at the top of her lungs. But that would have raised the suspicions of the Monitors. So she held back.

"First of all, do you know what a code is?" asked Arie.

"Of course I know what a coat is!" answered Jasmine. "A coat is what you wear over your clothes when it gets cold!"

"Oh, how I faint when I of you do listen," growled Arie. "I didn't say coat! I said code, c-o-d-e, farschteit?

Jasmine had no idea what a code was. Nor did she understand the meaning of farschteit. Perhaps it was the sound of a spider's sneeze?

"A code is a way for two creatures to communicate secretly without others understanding what they are saying. For example a simple *substitution code* is where you substitute one letter for another letter. Take a close look at my web. I spun a simple substitution code in which the A is replaced by the Z, the B is replaced by the Y etc. Go on, have a look!"

Jasmine looked carefully at the web. What she saw amazed her: two rows of letters side-by-side with a Z under an A, a Y under a B and so on:

A	B	C	D	E	F	G	H	I	J	K	L	M
Z	Y	X	W	V	U	T	S	R	Q	P	O	N

Because Arie's web wasn't wide enough, Arie spun a second set of rows that yielded the rest of the code:

N	O	P	Q	R	S	T	U	V	W	X	Y	Z
M	L	K	J	I	H	G	F	E	D	C	B	A

"Now read the message I spun for you," said Arie, "Can you make it out?" Jasmine saw BLF ZIV MRXV. Using her photographic memory she rapidly decoded the message and said, "Yes, it says that I'm nice!"

"Weary with the toil of spinning my web, I haste me to my nest. For thee and for myself no quiet find," growled Arie. "That's *not* what the message said!! It said that _you are nice_!"

"But that's what I said," complained Jasmine. "The message said that I'm nice."

"Oh, never mind," said Arie. "I think we both know what you mean. The main thing is that you understand the code and can decode secret messages that I and the other brother and sister spiders will leave for you. You will find these messages in different, unexpected places. If one of the Monitors sees you with a message, she will not be able to understand what the message says. When she asks you what the letters mean you will say that you are practicing your penmanship. Keep the code in your head. Do not disclose the code to anyone not even your closest friend. Follow the instructions in the code exactly. Meanwhile act as if nothing happened. It is supremely important that the Monitors do not know of your plans to escape. Are there any questions?"

It was now time for Jasmine to ask the two most important questions that had been on her mind since this conversation had started.

"My best friend is my doll Sochi. She is being punished for speaking out-of-turn and is being held prisoner in the DISCARDED ARTICLES ROOM, what they call the DAR around here. As much as I want to leave I cannot leave without Sochi. So whatever plans you make to help me escape, they must include Sochi."

"That shouldn't be too difficult," said Arie who was clearly touched by Jasmine's loyalty to her doll. Tears began to form in one of his simple eyes. "Anything else?" he asked.

92

"Yes Arie," said Jasmine. There are five other girls in the Sigma squad. They are all very nice, especially my new friend Cortina. I want you to help them escape also. Can you do it?"

Arie marveled at the loyalty shown by this young girl. But what Jasmine was asking was very difficult—impossible perhaps. There were obviously some things that Jasmine didn't understand; Arie would have to explain it to her at some point but now was not the time. "Look Jasmine," Arie said, "helping the other girls to escape presents all kind of problems. Let me think about it O.K? I will consult with the other brother and sister spiders and let you know O.K?"

Arie rubbed his long, his number one, pair of legs together. His pedipalps shook. "We've been talking long enough," he said. "It is time for you to get back to work and collect your daily quota of silk. Goodbye! Adios! Au revoir! A guten tag!"

20. First secret message

The day passed uneventfully. Jasmine could barely contain her excitement, now that the plan to escape was being hatched. However it was important to keep calm and Jasmine continued to work as if nothing unusual had taken place. Still, the day seemed endless. That evening's obedience session was led by Sister Fa, a poor choice in Jasmine's opinion because Sister Fa did not display the sharp insight of some of the other Monitors. Jasmine had learned a lot from Sister Wa's discussion and had hoped that Sister Wa would lead the obedience session again. But Sister Wa was not scheduled to do that until the following week. Jasmine remembered how Sister Fa gave silly answers to the charade game played by Sister La. Jasmine did not expect to learn very much.

The obedience session turned out to have been a waste of time. Sister Fa began by saying *Welcome grils. My name is Sister Gaga.* Sisters Re and Wa, who were standing by as members of the PVPIP, looked worried. After exchanging whispers with Sister Wa, Sister Re approached Sister Fa and whispered in her ear. Sister Fa blushed, shook her head in agreement and began again as: "Welcome girls. My name is Sister Fa. This evening I want to tell you about all the good things that happen to good grils—I mean girls— by which I mean girls that behave well and all the bad things that happen to bad girls by which I mean girls that behave badly."

Jasmine did not agree with what she heard. In her mind you could be a nice girl and still not be *too* well-behaved, and be a nasty girl and be *very* well-behaved. For example, Cortina was not all that well-behaved but was a nice girl: always helpful and kind. Jasmine knew a girl in school, whose name was Sangré Noir who was *very* well-behaved but never had a good thing to say about anyone or anything. She would never let you play with her toys and wouldn't lend you a thing. Worst of all, Sangré Noir was also mean to her dolls. In Jasmine's mind, Sangré Noir was not so nice.

On Sister Fa's desk were two stacks of posters, one on her left and one on her right. Each stack was covered with a silk cloth made from spider silk. Sister Fa's eyes were wide with excitement. The room had become so quiet that you could hear a feather drop. Suddenly she said: "Good girls get..." and then she removed a poster from the stack on the right, held it up to the class, and after a pause, read, "...DIAMONDS!" Sure enough, the poster showed a large diamond emitting rays of light.

All the girls pounded their tables with their fists in approval. Some yelled *Bravo!*

After a few seconds of quiet Sister Fa continued. "Bad girls get..." and then she removed a poster from the stack on the left, held it up to the class, and after a pause, read, "... DIRTY SOAPY WATER!" Sure enough, the poster showed a pail of dark soapy water. Once again the girls pounded the table tops with their fists. Some yelled *Niaah!*

After the third or fourth posters were unveiled, Sister Fa got the poster stacks mixed up. So she said, "Good girls get..." and then she pulled a poster from the stack on her left and read"... CARBUNCLES!" The poster showed a large, red, pus-filled pimple.

The girls were astounded. No sound came from them. Finally Jasmine heard Framboise giggling and whisper to no one in particular, "I am glad zat I am not zis good girl with the zit."

Sister Fa, who wasn't very smart, didn't realize what was going on. She believed everything she read and it never occurred to her that she had gotten the posters mixed up. So she went on. "Bad girls get..." and then she pulled a poster from the stack on her right and read "...CHOCOLOLATE ICE CREAM AND COOKIES!"

In one voice the girls yelled *Niaah!* Jasmine began to laugh. Chernobylia looked up; she had been drawing doodles of beets, pickles, sardines, and yogurt containers. Framboise whispered *I want to be like zat bad girl.* Cortina smiled at Jasmine and made a V sign with her fingers. Tossa de Mar whispered *What spazzatura is she giving us?* Sibasi whispered *Man that don't make no sense! Why the good girl get them pimples and the bad girl get the ice cream?*

Sisters Wa and Re, had not been paying attention to the classroom antics. They were silently going around the room trying to revive the dead and dying plants by giving them a liquid mixture of oxtail soup and calf's foot jelly. Every now and then you could hear a loud SPLAT as another shriveled and rotting plant keeled over and died. But when they heard the loud *Niaahs!* coming from the class the two Monitors looked up and quickly understood what was happening.

"The obedience session is over. Please line up and wait to be escorted back to your room." said Sister Re. The girls did as they were told. Jasmine joined the Sigma girls and waited for Sister Do. While waiting she noticed a little sticky piece of paper on her sleeve. She was about to crunch it up and throw it away but then she recalled Arie's warning: *You will find these messages in different, unexpected places.* She unfurled the little strip and read OLLP RM GSV XOLHVG RM BLFI ILLN. So Arie was at work, organizing the spiders at BEBE to help her escape! The thought that Arie had mobilized thousands of spiders trying to help her filled Jasmine's heart with joy.

Even before Sister Do appeared to take the Sigma girls back, Jasmine had decoded the message: *Look in the armoire in your room*!

21. Jasmine gets a map of BEBE and its surroundings

Back in her room, Jasmine had to work hard not to show her excitement. While the other girls were washing up, brushing their teeth, and getting into their pajamas, Jasmine went to the clothes closet and reached behind her things. Sure enough, there was a piece of paper there! When the other girls weren't looking, Jasmine took the paper to her bed and put it in the book she was reading *The Attack of the Salvenia Molesta*. The book described how this horrible water plant *Salvenia molesta* was suffocating all plant and fish life in all the fresh-water lakes around the world and how a brilliant young scientist named Jessica Qin-Chen was developing a chemical herbicide that could destroy the plant. Jessica was only 14 years old but already had a college degree in biology from Yael University. But now Jasmine's mind was not on the book but on the coded note she had removed from the closet. After washing, brushing her hair and teeth and putting on her pajamas Jasmine went to bed. She still had about 20 minutes before the lights went on. So she opened the book and made believe that she was reading it. But what she really was doing was decoding the message Arie had left for her.

Here is what the decoded message said:

Warning: Destroy as soon as you finish reading

Jasmine: Look at the map that goes with this message. It is a plan of the BEBE castle. The Sigma girls sleep in the East Tower but Sochi is locked in the DAR, which is in the Main Building. The dining hall, laundry, costumerie, infirmary, and obedience classes are in the Main Building also. The Main Building doesn't get locked because the Monitors sleep there.

There are six exits from BEBE. Only one gives you a reasonable chance to escape. That is the exit from the East Tower. Beware of the exit from the West Tower: it leads to a meadow full of poisonous plants. They give off a perfume which causes you to fall asleep for many years, maybe even centuries.

Do not use the exit from the West Wing. It leads to a cold, deep, black lake. You cannot swim across this lake because it is too cold. It is also full of cold-blooded water snakes that bite.

Definitely do not use the North Tower Exit. It leads to a hot desert full of large, yellow, poisonous scorpions. There are so many of them that they cover every square inch of ground. One sting from one of these scorpions will cause you to lose your memory. Two stings will cause you to forget how to speak. More than two stings and you will...Never mind it is best not to talk about it!

Above all avoid the South Tower and East Wing Exits. The South Tower Exit leads to Quicksand Manor a truly awful place! There is a house there that

96

emits good food smells. The smells attract hungry humans and spiders. However it is surrounded by quicksand traps, which have claimed the lives of many of our brother and sister spiders. Once you fall into a quicksand trap you cannot get out. You begin to sink, very slowly but steadily, towards the center of the Earth. And then you are never seen or heard from again! And while you are sinking into the quicksand there is this horrible laughter coming from the house.

The East Wing Exit leads perhaps to the worst place of all: the land of the sulfur pits! It is a dead and arid place with a hot black volcanic surface and many boiling sulfur pits. The air is so suffocating that after only two breaths you will faint. The sulfur pits are extremely deep. There is smoke and haze everywhere and you can't see where you are going. But the worst things of all are the little red-winged black devils that come crawling out of the sulfur pits to make mischief. They have black horns and red claws and talons instead of hands and feet. They can fly and they drag whoever is there into the sulfur pits. Among the learned spider elders, the place is known as the Forbidden Zone. They talk about the Forbidden Zone only in sign language by wiggling the tarsus joints of their legs. One of our brother spiders, who goes by the name of Dante, wrote a scary book about the place; he called the book Dante's Inferno.

That leaves the East Tower Exit. It leads to a large, dark forest. Beyond the forest there is a river and beyond the river there is a place called Magicland ruled over by a man known as Max the Magician. Like most Magicians, Max had hoped to become a cardiologist (a heart doctor) but couldn't afford to go to medical school. So he became a magician instead.
Max will help you get home if you recite the following verse:

> *Oy Vay, Oy vay, I have to say*
> *Help us, Max, to find our way*
> *If we get lost, I must confess*
> *We do not have a GPS!*

Study the map carefully and then destroy it and this message. Arie will give you more information when you see him tomorrow!

The work of decoding such a long message left Jasmine exhausted. By the time the lights went out Jasmine was fast asleep. But luckily she had not

PLAN of CASTLE BEBE
copyright by Arie Schnid

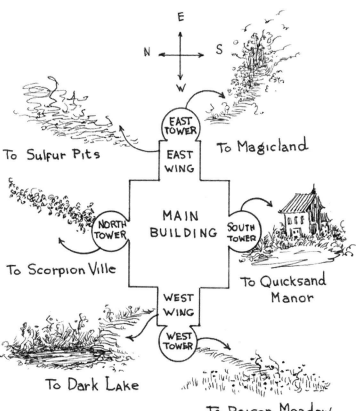

To Sulfur Pits

To Magicland

To Scorpion Ville

To Quicksand Manor

To Dark Lake

To Poison Meadow

forgotten the message's warning. She had torn up the message and the map into a thousand little pieces and flushed them down the toilet

22. Arie makes a plan for rescuing Sochi

The next day, at breakfast, Jasmine found a coded message under her glass of warm milk. *Amazing*, she thought, *there are spiders everywhere!* Meanwhile, there was to be no obedience class tonight. Instead the girls were going to be shown a movie as a reward for their good behavior. While the Sigma girls were talking excitedly about the movie they were to see that evening—something called *The Triumph of Friggy the Frog*—Jasmine dropped the little piece of paper in her lap. So quick and deft was this maneuver that none of the girls had any inkling that it even took place. When Jasmine glanced down to see what the message said she read:

R MVVW GL GZOP GL BLF ZH HLLM ZH KLHHRYOV./ZIRV

Jasmine had gotten very good at decoding these messages. She could do it without using a pencil and paper. She almost immediately read *I need to talk to you as soon as possible. / Arie.* She figured this had to be important since she was going to see Arie later anyway during her silk-collecting duties. She resolved that once she got to the attic, she would immediately go to A6 R9 and talk to Arie.

After breakfast, the girls were led back to their room and changed into their work clothes. Soon Sister Do came to lead them to the attic to begin work. As soon as Jasmine reached the attic she went to see Arie. He greeted her with:

"What is your substance, whereof are you made,
That millions of strange shadows on you tend?
Since every one hath, every one, one shade,
And you, but one, can every shadow lend."

Reader: Arie is a well-educated spider who can quote the great poet and playwright William Shakespeare. In these lines he ponders aloud what Jasmine is really like.

Jasmine had no idea what Arie was talking about but it sounded mysterious. She liked the sound of what he said; it had something to do with millions of shadows and a window shade. Maybe her mother could tell her what it meant.

"Where did you learn to talk like that?" asked Jasmine with interest.

Arie wiggled his pedipalps. "My mother was something of a scholar," he said. "She had me take private lessons with a tutor whom she called the 'dark lady'. I never found out what the 'dark lady's' real name was, but she was a good teacher. She's the one who taught me how to talk like that."

"But we are getting off the subject," continued Arie. "There are some important things I need to tell you. My spider friends did some investigative work and agreed that with a little luck we should be able to get you, Sochi, and Cortina out of here in the next few days."

"But that's fantastic!" exclaimed Jasmine. "How about the other Sigma girls?"

"Well there the news is not so good. It appears that my friends don't think that getting Sibasi, Framboise, Tossa de Mar, and Chernobylia out now is a good idea."

"But why?" asked Jasmine. "Surely if you can get Cortina and me out you can get them out also!"

"Look," said Arie, all simple eyes now sternly focused. "There are some things that you don't understand. BEBE is not a pleasant place but it isn't all bad either. For some young girls a brief stay in BEBE will actually help them later in life. It didn't exactly hurt Golda Meier, Margaret Thatcher, and Hillary Clinton to have spent some time here did it? But let's talk about your friends shall we? Take Sibasi for example. She is learning to control her aggression and by the time her mother Mykishka comes to pick her up in two week's time she'll be more obedient and have a more pleasant personality. It was because of your desire to see your friends go free that we went through the trouble of writing Mykishka a letter to pick up her daughter in two weeks. You should feel proud!"

"In the case of Chernobylia," Arie continued, "she really had no business giving her little brother sardines that made him glow in the dark. But here is the good news. My spy Frank Lycosa crawled into the file cabinet and read her file and found out that her parents are coming to get her in ten days. It seems that Chernobylia really feels remorse for what she did and has promised to be well-behaved. So you don't have to worry about her!"

"Well, what about Framboise and Tossa de Mar?" asked Jasmine.

"Aha!" said Arie. "I knew that you would ask about them! Well you will be pleased to know that these two girls have written letters of apology to their parents. Their parents have become friends with each other and they are coming here in nine days to get the girls out. Framboise and Tossa de Mar have made great progress. Henri and Janine, Framboise's parents, and Giuseppe and Octavia, Tossa de Mar's parents are taking the girls for a one week vacation to Disney World. But not one word of this to any of the girls! What I'm telling you is in absolute confidence!"

This news came as great relief to Jasmine. She had been worried that these poor girls would spend the rest of their lives in BEBE. But in fact, in two weeks time, they would all be out. Jasmine was happy that she was able to help, even if only a little.

"Which brings me to you and Cortina," said Arie. "I think that after Sister Wa's obedience class, you now understand why you sometimes get into trouble; there is no need for you to stay in BEBE any longer. That's why we agreed to help you escape. In Cortina's case she really didn't do anything that bad. She didn't mean to give the poopin' pills to Uncle Harry and the sleeping pills to Ragweed. One of the sister spiders in Scotland, who lives in Uncle Harry's basement and knows how to use the *internet*, send us a message in which she described Uncle Harry as a sourpuss who doesn't like kids. Ragweed is a lazy horse whose problem is that he sleeps all day and eats too much and that's why he ain't poopin'.""

Arie signaled for Jasmine to come closer. "The first thing that you must do is to free Sochi from the DAR. This must be done at night because during the day the Monitors turn on some kind of electronic gizmo that rings like crazy when you open the door to the DAR unless you dial-in some numbers on an electronic key pad. The Monitors were talked into buying this so-called 'electric eye' by three weird creatures that called themselves Tilops and ran an insurance company called Fleece, Flimflam and 'Stool', Inc. The Tilops told the Monitors that the electric eye would provide insurance against theft. At night the Monitors turn off the electric eye because they figure that all the girls are asleep; then they lock the door with a cheap lock that is easily opened with a pin. The electric eye requires a lot of electricity to operate and the Monitors figure they can save money by turning it off at night, which is pretty stupid if you ask me. I mean what's the point of putting in a theft prevention device if you're not going to use it. At night there are only two PVPIP Monitors on patrol: usually these are Sisters Mi and Fa but there could be others. Sister Fa is not the brightest star in the constellation if you know what I mean. But Sister Mi is very sharp. If she catches you you will have a lot of explaining to do!"

Jasmine already knew about Sister Fa. But she knew nothing about Sister Mi except that she had a kind face. Jasmine was shrewd enough to know that a kind face didn't mean that she was a kind person. What was it that her mother had taught her? *That you can't tell a book by its cover!*

Arie continued with his instructions. "The DAR is on the third floor of the main building. To get there you and Cortina will have to leave your room, take the elevator down to the main east-west hallway, and cross the East Wing until you get to the Main building. Then you will take the stairs up to the third floor and rescue Sochi."

A loud: *Jasmine, I need to talk to you!* came from the door. Jasmine was surprised to see Sister Do there. Had Sister Do seen Jasmine talking to Arie? Was the escape caper already in ruins because she, Jasmine, stupidly failed to watch who was listening? Jasmine tried to hide her nervousness as she went to Sister Do.

"How come you are spending so much time with the web at A6 R9?" asked a frowning Sister Do, tickle stick in hand. "At this rate you will never make your daily quota. And you know what that means: no movie for you tonight and a re-education session with Sister Re. You wouldn't want that would you?"

If Jasmine had one solid talent it was her ability to concoct stories and excuses faster than anyone on this planet. In fact Jasmine sometimes worried that there was a second personality living in her body that did nothing all day long except cook up excuses and tall tales.

"I was examining the A6 R9 web so see why it was so ragged and small. I know that it is very important for the Sisters to have all the silk they need to make the shoes for their delicate feet. I was trying to coax the spider in A6 R9 out of his nest to see if there was something the matter with him. Perhaps a stay in the Spider Retreat Room (SRR) will make him more productive?"

These words mollified Sister Do. She was happy to hear that Jasmine took a professional interest in her work. Her suggestion that the A6 R9 spider be given some time off in the SRR was a good one. However Sister Do recalled that the last time the tenant at A6 R9 was in the SRR, he turned the place upside down and behaved outrageously. The 72 dark-eyed, adoring, *Pholcus phalangioides* (daddy longlegs) wept for a week after he left. Even now the *phalangioides* talk about the A6 R9 spider as if he were some kind of god with incredible energy.

"You needn't worry about him," said Sister Do. "He will soon get the vacation he's entitled to. Meanwhile my dear you should hurry and complete your work. I wouldn't want you to miss the movie this evening."

When Jasmine heard these soft words she knew she was off the hook. She had to get back to work. She would talk to Arie later.

23. The escape plan goes into effect

In the afternoon work detail, Jasmine avoided A6 R9 except to tell Arie about the brief conversation she had with Sister Do. As usual Arie greeted her in words that she didn't understand.

"Good Yontiff, Pontiff!" Arie said. "What's on the menu today?"
"What does that mean?" asked Jasmine who was slightly irritated by Arie's demeanor. This was no time to talk funny!

"Sorry!" said Arie. "That's a punch line from a joke that my uncle told at Thanksgiving dinner. His wife *Lycosa sculata* (wolf spider) had heard the joke so often that she became hysterical and ate him on the spot! So much for 'to have and to hold 'til death do us part.'"

"Never mind punch lines from stupid jokes!" said an exasperated Jasmine. "What do we do after we rescue Sochi? How do we get out of BEBE?"

Arie turned serious. "I have written the whole escape plan in code. You will find it at the bottom of the armoire in your room, along with some things that you and Cortina will need to escape. But we better break-off. I think I see Sister Do by the door and she is looking this way."

Jasmine knew that with his simple eyes Arie would not have been able to see Sister Do by the door. He was gently warning her that it was not a good idea to be seen together. Jasmine took the hint. "O.K.," she said. "I'll see you later."

Jasmine had no trouble collecting her daily quota of spider silk. When the workday was over Jasmine and the other girls returned to their room to rest. In the bottom of the armoire, Jasmine found a long coded message hidden in one of her books. Under the pretext of resting on her bunk and reading *The Attack of the Salvenia Molesta*, Jasmine decoded the message. This is what it said:

Warning: Destroy as soon as you finish reading

The door to Sochi's room will have to be unlocked but that will be easy to do with the pin we left you in the armoire. Fortunately the electric eye that shields the door during the day will be turned off. Once you have Sochi, you and Cortina will retrace your steps back to the main east-west hallway, past the East Wing and back to the East Tower. Once you get to the East Tower do not return to your room! Avoid the elevator altogether and walk down two flights of stairs to the East Tower Exit. The exit door is not marked Exit! Instead, to confuse girls that might be tempted to escape, the Monitors have put up a scary sign that says

Warning; keep away
This room contains the dangerous machinery that makes the calf's foot jelly.

You and Cortina will ignore the sign. The exit door will be locked with a combination lock. I've got Frank Lycosa crawling around the inside of the lock now to determine what the combination is. Frank is good at that sort of thing. He used to work for the crime syndicate as a lock maven. The combination to the lock will be left for you in the armoire after this evening's movie.

Once you leave BEBE do not turn back! You will hear weird sounds urging you to return. Do not listen to them. Hurry along the path until you get to the forest. The forest is very dark and to guide your way you will use the flashlight in the package that will be left for you at the bottom of the armoire. It took 7259 of my fellow spiders to schlep that package from here to your armoire.

It should take you about ten hours to cross the forest. Then you will cross a stream called Spoon River and enter Magicland. After that, Max the magician will help you get back home.

Remember all that Arie did for you (and I'm not even your mother!). Write and call sometime when you get back home. And remember to eat a good, healthy breakfast every morning and don't hang out with hoodlums.

Good luck. I shall miss you (sob).

Love/ Arie

It suddenly occurred to Jasmine that if everything went well she would not see Arie again; tears came to her eyes. She hadn't known Arie for long but he had become her good friend and she trusted him. In fact even though he was only a spider she trusted him more that her human friends Dorvit and Pilata. For some strange reason he reminded her of her mother: the advice that he gave her was not that different from that of her mother's; for example *'Eat a good healthy breakfast every morning'*. Wasn't that just the kind of thing that her mother might say! Jasmine toyed with the idea of taking Arie with her. But what kind of life would Arie have in Lalaville, where everybody was always calling those exterminator people with the white helmets and spray tanks to kill insects and spiders? Moreover Sochi was afraid of spiders and would also become very jealous if she knew that Jasmine brought home this dear, non-human, friend. Sochi took pride in the fact that she was Jasmine's best non-human friend. And where would Arie live in Lalaville? If he lived in the house, the exterminator people would get him and if he lived outside one of the hornet wasps that Arie was so afraid of would get him.

No! It didn't make good sense to take Arie with her! Leaving him behind was the right thing to do but it was one of the most difficult decisions that Jasmine ever made. Arie had a good life at BEBE, with medical insurance and regular vacations in the Spider Retreat Room. She would just have to get used to life without Arie. Besides Arie probably wouldn't want to go anyway.

At five o'clock the girls went through their routine of cleaning up and preparing for dinner. They were glad that instead of obedience class after dinner they were going to see a movie. The DING-DONG of the dinner bell reminded them that the dinner hour had arrived. As usual Sister Do led them to the dinning hall. As they walked through the various corridors, Jasmine tried to remember every detail of what she saw. Her photographic memory would come in handy when she had to navigate these halls later in the darkness.

The girls were given the usual steaming bowl of tomato puree with white kidney beans. But instead of the calf's foot jelly they were expecting for desert they each got a large slice of apple pie. Wow! This was a very pleasant surprise! The apple pie wasn't even bad and Jasmine, who had a sweet tooth, was prepared to eat the whole thing. But then she recalled what was in Arie's message: *It should take you about ten hours to cross the forest.* If she ate the whole thing now she would have nothing to eat during their ten hours in the forest.

She turned to Cortina who was sitting next to her and whispered, "Don't eat the whole slice. Save some for later." Cortina, who hadn't yet been told of the escape plans for later that night, looked at Jasmine in surprise. "But why?" she whispered back.

Now was not the time to talk about the escape. "Just trust me," whispered Jasmine. "Put what you don't finish in a napkin and take it back to the room later. Believe me— it is very important to do as I say."

Like the other Sigma girls, Cortina had been very impressed with the way Jasmine had handled Waxface and the Tilops. She trusted Jasmine's judgment and leadership skills; if Jasmine said to save some of the pie that was good enough for her. The explanation could wait until later.

It was Arie who had told Jasmine to wait until the last moment before telling Cortina about the escape. "The less anyone knows about the escape, the better," he had said. "Cortina is a bright girl but she may talk in her sleep. Tell her about the escape only when you make your move. "

Dinner was over. After all the dishes were put away, the girls were asked to move their chairs so that they all faced the front of the room. Jasmine estimated that there were nearly 200 girls there.

The Monitors went around turning off the bare bulbs hanging over each of the tables. After a while it got pretty dark inside the dining hall except for two exit lights and a strange bluish light that seemed to be coming from the floor. Jasmine had noticed this light before in the halls and larger rooms in BEBE. It came from a narrow depression in the floor and once your eyes got adjusted to it, you could make your way all over BEBE even when all the other lights were out. It occurred to Jasmine that she could use the map furnished by Arie and the blue floor light to find her way out of BEBE when the time came to make her escape.

The girls all watched the blank screen in anticipation of seeing the movie. Sister Wa climbed up on one of the tables in the front. "Dear girls," she began, "this evening you will see an inspiring film by the Swedish director Indebar Boreman about a little frog that succeeded in life despite considerable adversity. Abandoned by his mother when merely a tadpole, Friggy the frog had to combat prejudice, ignorance and apathy to survive. But by sheer will and strength of character Friggy not only survived but became the head of a multimillion dollar corporation that specializes in gourmet foods for frogs, toads, tropical fishes, and other insignificant household pets. We here at BEBE hope that this film will inspire you to be '*all that you can be.*'"

When Sister Wa was finished with her little speech, she climbed off the table with the help of Sister Mi and the movie began. It showed Friggy as a little tadpole swimming in a murky pond and being bumped into by bigger tadpoles. "Whatsamatter you little runt? Haven't learned how to swim yet?" said a larger bully tadpole, which caused his tadpole friends to laugh loudly. Later it showed Friggy in school asking his teacher, "Dear Mr. Axelrod: What's the difference between ignorance and apathy?" and Mr. Axelrod turning red in the face and yelling at poor Friggy, "I don't know and I don't care!"

Still later the movie showed Friggy in a fancy college where he is the only frog in the class. Having been admitted in a special program that admits a small number of frogs, horses and mules from disadvantaged backgrounds, Friggy feels out of place in this world of humans. For one thing he cannot learn to wear loafers without socks. Friggy joins the campus debate club and learns to sharpen his debating skills. He wins a key debate, taking the *yes* position on the question *Should Diet Dr. Brown's Soda be universally available to all Americans?* His debating skills attract lots of girl students who kiss him hoping that he'll turn into a prince. When this doesn't happen, they turn away from him in disgust.

Friggy graduates from college with *high honors*. He moves to New York City where he is friendless and alone. One day while hopping through the rain in Central Park he is chased by a man in a tuxedo and top hat and a woman wearing a long white gown and a diamond necklace. They catch him using the man's top hat as a net and bring him back to their fourteen-room apartment on Park Avenue. He is put in a large glass tank with other frogs and small animals and hears himself called a *Living Art Tableau.*

While there, Friggy becomes friendly with the couple's daughter, Fortuna, who has a really stupid dog called Faunus that thinks that everything in the world is a fire hydrant. Fortuna protects Friggy from Faunus and introduces him to her two best doll friends Heather and Hilton. Friggy is not unhappy in this strange household but is forced to eat a bland diet of iceberg lettuce and tofu. Friggy wonders why there isn't better food available for frogs.

One day a new frog is added to the *Living Art Tableau.* The new frog's name is Daniel Tramp and he's got a huge amount of money to invest. Friggy tells him about his idea for gourmet food for small, insignificant pets. Tramp is impressed and invites Friggy to form a partnership but there is a problem: how will they escape from the tank?

Friggy has an idea for escaping. One day when there is no one home except for Faunus, Friggy yells *Fire! The End is Near! Save Yourself!* Faunus—who is a coward—panics and runs around in circles knocking everything over including the glass tank holding Friggy, Tramp, and all the other insignificant small creatures in it. In no time at all they all escape. When the owners get back they are very upset with Faunus and send him to the doghouse.

Friggy and Tramp form a company called *Tasty Treats for Tiny Things*, Inc. The company makes millions of dollars. Friggy gives money to charity and runs for a seat in the United States Senate. He becomes the first elected frog in United States history. Pretty soon he is invited to join the prestigious Senate Select Subcommittee of Non-Human Senators. There he meets several powerful snakes, vultures, rats, and horses' behinds. The last scene shows him happily going to work in a chauffeur-driven car wearing a top hat and smoking a large cigar. End of story!

When the movie was over, the Monitors turned the lights back on. Many of the girls had fallen asleep and others looked bleary-eyed. Clearly the movie was not a great success. Jasmine found the movie dull and unrealistic. For example where did Tramp get all that money in the first place? And why did the college girls think that Friggy would turn into a prince if they kissed him?

Jasmine hadn't seen the movie before but somehow various scenes seemed familiar. Where in the past had she heard about the well-dressed couple and Faunus and Fortuna and Heather and Hilton? Jasmine couldn't recall but it didn't matter; right now the only thing that mattered was to carry out the escape plan.

It was nearly eight o'clock in the evening when Jasmine and the other girls were led back to their room by Sister Do. The sleepy girls went through their evening rituals of washing up, brushing their teeth, and getting into their pajamas like zombies. While the other girls were busy with these activities, Jasmine went to the armoire and looked into the deepest, darkest corner of the bottom shelf. Sure enough what she found there made her heart race: a flashlight, a strip of paper with numbers, and a short coded message.

When no one was looking Jasmine removed the pillow cover from her pillow and put the flashlight and the left-over slice of apple pie in it. Having no knapsack to carry the things that she needed, Jasmine intended to use the pillow cover as a substitute. She didn't like taking things that didn't belong to her but this was an emergency. When (and if) she got home she would mail the pillow cover back to BEBE with a note of apology.

After decoding the message, Jasmine read:

Frank Lycosa figured out the combination number of the lock on the exit door. He's written it down on the little strip of paper that you found.

Wake Cortina around one o'clock in the morning; then go to the DAR to rescue Sochi. Retrace your steps to the East Tower Exit. By then it should be around two o'clock. Unlock the exit door and leave quietly. Keep Sochi quiet. Word has gotten around that she is a big talker and doesn't know when to quit jabbering.

Once you and Cortina and Sochi are outside, do not look back. There is a rumor that anyone who looks back turns into salt but I've never heard it happen.

There may be Craxies in the forest so be on the lookout for them. Avoid them at all costs!

You should get to Magicland by ten o'clock in the morning. Max will help you from there on.

Good luck and goodbye (sob)!

Arie Schnid

PS: I include a picture of me so that you'll remember me. The picture was taken about a year ago. I'm much grayer now. It is because of my children: they don't write, they don't phone...I worry about them so!

Arie Schnid

Jasmine looked at the strip of paper with the combination. It said:

09-66-06

Jasmine put the put the strip of paper in the plastic bag. The combination was easy to remember but Jasmine didn't want to take a chance on her memory alone. She looked at Cortina who was already asleep. It was time for Jasmine to sleep also; she would need all the rest she could get for the coming night's trials.

24. Escape from BEBE

Jasmine is walking on a sunless rocky hillside in a freezing drizzle. There are no flowers or grasses or live trees to be seen anywhere. Every so often there is a gnarled dead tree with one or two crows perching on one of its denuded branches. She is very cold and has no idea where she is going. But she knows that she has to keep moving if she is to survive. There are no houses or roads or lights or even road signs to be seen anywhere. She is all alone and doesn't remember where she left Sochi. Suddenly she spots two unshaven, homeless men sitting on a dirty boulder. Their names are Vladimir and Estragon. She asks them for help but they chase her away. They are waiting for someone or something called *Godot*, they say, and *Godot* will not come if Jasmine is there. Jasmine has no idea who or what *Godot* is. Soon Jasmine loses sight of the men.

Jasmine is starving and looks in her bag to retrieve some food. But the bag has a hole in it and the food must have fallen out. In the distance Jasmine sees lightning bolts and very dark rain clouds. She must get home before the violent thunderstorm hits. Suddenly Jasmine becomes aware that she is being watched; she becomes very frightened. Up ahead she sees the back of a signpost. Maybe the signpost will tell her where she is and give directions to her home in Lalaville. Jasmine rushes up to the signpost to read its message. What she reads causes her to cringe with fear.

Beware of Craxies

If ever you are standing where
You're bound to meet a craxie

You'd better beat it out of there
By boat or bus or taxi.

Though craxies neither scratch nor bite,
A craxie's not a saint
He'll glue your fingers, hold them tight,
And cover you with paint.

Jasmine falls to the ground sobbing. But the ground is not hard: it is soft and white. Jasmine realizes that she is in her bunk and that she has been dreaming!

It took Jasmine a few minutes to recover from this horrible nightmare. What did it mean? Jasmine remembered that in her father's book collection there was a thick book by a Doctor Sigmund Freud, which was called *The Interpretation of Dreams*. She wished that she had the book with her now; maybe it would help her understand what the dream was all about. Who put this stupid and scary dream into her head anyway? She couldn't blame Dorvit or any of her other friends because they were not around.

Jasmine looked at her watch: it was just one o'clock. Jasmine saw that Cortina was fast asleep; it was time to wake her. With a gentle shake Jasmine woke Cortina and signaled her not to speak. Cortina trusted her friend and did as she was told. Jasmine gave Cortina a note on which she had written *Dear Cortina: Please stay quiet until we leave this room. We are going to escape from BEBE but first we have to rescue Sochi. When we leave this room we can talk in whispers. I have the map of BEBE in my head and I memorized the way out. Take along all the things that you will need to survive a night in a cold forest. If we run into one of the Monitors let me do the talking. If everything goes according to plan we should be out of here in about one hour. Don't forget to take the apple pie. And above all stay very quiet until we leave this room. If we wake the others we shall not be able to escape. Trust me! I have good friends among the spiders of BEBE and they have done a lot of work to help us escape.*

Cortina read the note with the help of the flashlight that Arie's friends had left in the closet. When she was done she indicated to Jasmine that she understood the contents of the note and gave Jasmine a big, happy, smile. Then she pointed to the other four sleeping girls but Jasmine shook her head to say *no, we can't take them*. Later Jasmine would explain to her that Arie and his friends could not risk allowing the other girls to escape as well; besides the other girls would soon be free anyway.

Some of the girls were talking in their sleep. Jasmine could hear Framboise murmur "Araignée du matin:chagrin!" (**reader**: this is French for *see a spider in the morning and you will have a bad day*!). Tossa de Mar was whispering "Cerco un regalo per mia madre!" (**reader**: this is Italian for *I'm looking for a present for my mother*!). Sibasi was humming "♩ I shall not escape/ BEBE is my fate/Big Sister is my guide/ Big Sister's on my side. Oooh, Oooh, Oooh,...♩".

But this was no time to listen in on the private conversations the girls were having with themselves. It was time to go. The flashlight was turned off and the girls quietly left the room. Almost immediately Jasmine's eyes got accustomed to the narrow blue light coming out from the lighting strip in the ground. As Jasmine closed the door she felt a twinge of great sadness: she probably wouldn't see Sibasi, Tossa de Mar, Chernobylia, and Framboise again. She had grown very fond of these brave and loyal companions. In her heart she wished them a happy life and for a moment reconsidered whether she really wanted to escape and leave them behind. But Sochi, Cortina, and most important—her parents—had to come first. Once the door was closed there was no turning back; besides Arie and his friends would look out for the remaining girls.

Jasmine and Cortina had reached the elevator. For a second Jasmine considered taking the stairs instead. The elevator was quiet but you could still hear the hum of its motor when the car was moving. On the other hand they were at least 300 feet above the east-west hallway and taking the stairs would tire them out and waste a lot of time. So Jasmine opted for the elevator and within seconds they had reached the east-west hallway. So far so good! Walking on their tiptoes Jasmine and Cortina crossed the East Wing and reached the Main Hall. Somewhere in the darkness they could hear the snoring of the Monitors. They heard other noises as well: the flushing of a toilet and the creaking of a door. As Jasmine peered into the darkness she could make out a small moving circle of light. Panic gripped her heart! Was this a ghost? Had they already been discovered? Was it some sort of device that was tracking them?

It was Cortina however who figured out what it was: one of the Monitors was doing her nightly rounds with a small flashlight. They had not been discovered! But now they would have to be extra careful since the slightest noise would give them away.

Soon the circle of light got fainter and finally vanished altogether. The Monitor must have gone into another part of the building.

A few minutes later they reached the Main Hall's central staircase. This was the trickiest part of the whole escape plan: they had to walk up three flights of steep stairs, force the lock to the DAR, remove Sochi, and—most difficult of all—keep Sochi quiet.

They reached the DAR without difficulty and listened for any sounds. Behind the door they could hear someone talking in the tone of a queen addressing her subjects. "Yes," the voice said, "I have no interest in leading a small, trivial, monotonous life as other dolls do. It is high adventure that I seek! Single-handedly I defeated the fearsome ogre called Waxface and saved my mistress Jasmine. Without regard for my life I rescued her from the clutches of those most-awful of creatures—the Tilops. And now, while she is hiding and whimpering somewhere in this building, I am already making plans to take-on the most formidable enemy of kids and dolls on this planet: the Craxies!"

No one talked like that except Sochi! At first Jasmine was overcome with joy to know that Sochi was alive and well. But then, as her brain processed what she had just heard, she had half a mind to leave Sochi in the DAR and escape with Cortina only. But Jasmine bit her tongue; now was not the time to give in to her irritation with Sochi. She removed the pin from her sack and inserted it into the lock. A quick twist and the lock opened. Jasmine was amazed: did she have a natural talent for opening locked doors? Was there some way she could put this talent to use without getting into trouble with the police? She would have to think about that when she got back home—if she got back home.

Jasmine opened the door as quietly as she could and shined her flashlight on the floor in the center of the room. There was Sochi surrounded by—perhaps as many as— twenty dolls who listened with rapt concentration to Sochi's monologue. The slight air disturbance created by the opening of the door caused Sochi to turn her head towards Jasmine and Cortina. If she was pleased to see Jasmine or even recognized her, she gave no hint of having done so. Instead she said in a somewhat supercilious tone, "Please do not disturb me while I describe my adventures to those unfortunates whose lives have been routine and dull. Sit or stand quietly until I'm done!"

That's it! fumed Jasmine, *I've had enough of this nonsense!* She rushed into the room, grabbed Sochi by the arm and quickly stuck her into the pillow case. "One sound out of you and so help me I'll turn you over to Big Sister who will use your stuffing to wipe her silk shoes!" she hissed. "Not a sound, not a word, from you until we get out of here!"

Sochi knew that she had gone too far. Jasmine was risking her liberty, possibly her life, to save Sochi and here was Sochi showing no respect or gratitude. She retreated into Jasmine's sweater and whispered. "I'm sorry! I was overcome listening to my stories about my heroism!" This caused Jasmine to sneer, "I'm so sorry that you were overcome by your 'heroism'. When we get home we'll have to discuss this 'heroism' of yours. *Meanwhile*, you will be *so* quiet that I won't even hear the strands of your stuffing rubbing together!"

Jasmine and Cortina quietly left the room and locked the door. This way the monitors would not know that anything was amiss. Had they left the door unlocked the Monitor on patrol would have known that something was going on. Still Jasmine felt a little bad for the other dolls in the DAR. She hoped that when the Sigma girls were released they wouldn't forget to reclaim their dolls.

Except for the weak blue light in the floor everything was dark. The girls retraced their steps down the three steep flights of stairs. Once more they could hear the snoring of the Monitors coming from somewhere on the ground floor of the main building. The small, moving, circle of light they had seen earlier was nowhere to be seen now. So far so good, but Jasmine was nervous: this was all a little too easy.

They had just entered the East Wing when Jasmine once more heard the creaking of a door. *Doors don't creak by themselves*, Jasmine thought. *Someone is walking around checking the doors and halls!* Jasmine had an overwhelming urge to turn on the flashlight to see what was going on. If truth be told, she was close to panicking. But she couldn't afford to panic because Cortina's and Sochi's freedom depended on her keeping a cool head. So she took a deep breath and whispered to Cortina, "One or more of the Monitors are roaming around. We have to be extra careful if we're not going to be discovered."

Jasmine could sense a very slight air disturbance as she tip-toed across the floor of the East Wing. *Perhaps someone opened a door or a window somewhere,* she thought. As she looked back to see if Cortina was keeping up, Jasmine bumped into something soft! *I don't remember there being anything here when we first came out to save Sochi,* Jasmine thought. Suddenly she was blinded by the beam of a flashlight shining right into her face. She could hear Sochi moan from fear in the pillow case. Cortina looked as if she was going to faint.

"Why hello grils, oops, I mean girls," said the Monitor holding the flashlight. "Looks like I caught you trying to escape," the voice croaked. "You know what this means: thirty re-education sessions for each one of you, solitary confinement for ten days, no participation in movies or games, no deserts, and a doubling of the time that you will spend in BEBE. And that miserable doll that you are hiding in the pillow cover will be immediately shipped out to that nice Dr. Priam who runs the Pandora Circus Company. I'm sure that he'll find a nice place for her!" An unpleasant cackle followed this little speech.

Jasmine's heart was beating so fast and hard that she was afraid that it would tear itself out of her chest. Meanwhile Jasmine's arm was going numb from the panicky grip that Cortina had on her arm. If Cortina had not been able to grip Jasmine's arm she would have fainted outright. Desperate as the situation was, Jasmine saw one tiny ray of light: even without being able to see who was holding the flashlight, Jasmine figured out that it was Sister Fa. Wasn't it at one of the obedience sessions that Sister Fa had stumbled over the word *girls* and had said *grils*? Jasmine's mind went into overdrive; she had to find a way out of this situation quickly because Sister Fa was getting ready to alert the other Monitors and once they got into the act it would be all over: the escape would have failed!

"Dear Sister Fa," Jasmine said. "You are seeing an apparition, a mirage! There is no one here except you. Think of how ridiculous you will look when you call the other Sisters and they come and find no one here. The sooner you turn off this stupid flashlight and go about your business, the better it will be for your reputation!"

During the brief time that Sister Fa was joyously listing all the terrible things that would happen to the trio, Jasmine, somewhat unconsciously, had concocted a desperate plan. She was going to take advantage that Sister Fa was—to say it as charitably as possible—not too bright.

"What are talking about?" said an incredulous Sister Fa. "You and Cortina, and that miserable creature Sochi are standing right in front of me! I can hear you talking and breathing! How can you be a mirage?"

"Dear Sister Fa," Jasmine said. "Do you believe in logic?"

"Of course I believe in logic," said Sister Fa. "Logic is what makes the world go round!"

Suddenly Jasmine felt a twinge of pity for Sister Fa. She had always heard from Caesar and Chacha that *love* makes the world go round. Perhaps Sister Fa never experienced any love and therefore thought that *logic* makes the world go round. But now was not the time to feel sorry for anyone except herself, Cortina, and Sochi.

"Dear Sister Fa," Jasmine said. "If I could prove to you *logically* that we are not here and that therefore you are seeing an apparition, would you go about your business quietly and leave us alone?"

"Of course, I would leave you alone if you are not here!" said a suspicious Sister Fa. "But how are you going to logically convince me that you are an apparition?"

Jasmine's confidence had grown during this interchange with Sister Fa. There was a good chance that she might pull this off.

"Sister Fa," Jasmine asked, "Are we in Africa?"

"Of course not!" said Sister Fa with a sneer.

"Sister Fa," Jasmine asked, "Are we in Brazil?"

"A stupid question," said Sister Fa. Of course you aren't in Brazil!"

"Sister Fa," Jasmine asked, "Are we on the South Pole?"

"What kind of a game are you playing?" said Sister Fa with some confidence. "Of course you are not on the South Pole!"

Jasmine was now ready to deliver the master stroke. She hoped with all her heart that it would work!

"Sister Fa," Jasmine said. "If we are not in Africa, Brazil, or the South Pole, we must be somewhere else, right?"

"That's right!" said Sister Fa triumphantly. "You must be somewhere else."

"Please say it again, dear Sister Fa," said Jasmine. "We must be somewhere else!"

"That's right, my poor little Jasmine," said Sister Fa. "You must be somewhere else! Maybe the stress of having been caught trying to escape has affected your ability to think!"

"But Sister Fa," Jasmine said quietly, "If we are somewhere else we can't be here, isn't that correct?"

"Of course you can't be here if you are somewhere else!" said a confident Sister Fa.

"So you see Sister Fa, since we are not here you are seeing an apparition!" whispered Jasmine. "It is best that you go now and reflect on what brought on this apparition. Perhaps you have been working too hard."

Sister Fa was now completely bewildered. After a few moments she said very quietly, "You are right of course. If you are somewhere else you can't be here. Perhaps I have been working too hard. Please promise me that you will not tell the other Sisters that I am prone to seeing apparitions. Perhaps some rest and a visit to the infirmary will cure me of seeing apparitions. I am so sorry that I bothered you. Goodbye."

"You have my solemn word that I will tell no one about your apparitions. Goodbye Sister Fa and may the Force be with you." Jasmine finally relaxed as she saw Sister Fa walk away hesitantly into the darkness. She would not have to worry about Sister Fa anymore.

When Cortina realized that Jasmine had saved them she gave her a grateful hug. Sochi, who had heard the whole conversation, spoke from the pillowcase in a weak voice. "Tell me Jasmine," Sochi said, "if we are not here where are we then?" Jasmine and Cortina repressed a tremendous urge to laugh. "Never mind," whispered Jasmine, "I'll explain it to you later. Meanwhile stay quiet. We still have to make our way to the exit without being caught." But Sochi had to have the last word. "It's a good thing for that nincompoop Sister Fa that we are not here. I was beginning to lose my temper and you know how dangerous I get when I'm angry!"

The girls followed the weak blue light through the East Wing. Before them stood the entrance to the East Tower and beyond that was... freedom! By now they were too far from the Main Hall to hear the Sisters' snoring. It was so quiet that you could hear your own breathing! As they tiptoed through the East Tower entrance they suddenly heard a voice coming from behind one of the stone columns holding up the East Tower. The girls were so frightened they jumped into the air. Jasmine's hair stood straight up; Cortina went white as a sheet. Sochi went limp.

"Jasmine, please hand me the pillowcase that you are carrying," the voice said.

Jasmine held up the pillowcase and it was taken by whoever was behind the stone column. Jasmine nearly fainted when she realized that Arie's last note was in the pillow case. Whoever was going to examine the contents of the pillowcase was surely going to find it and realize that the girls were planning to escape. But wait! The note was in code so its message could not be deciphered unless you knew the code.

Jasmine was already thinking up an explanation of why she and Cortina and Sochi were walking around BEBE at nearly two o'clock in the morning. She would say that they couldn't sleep and had taken a walk to tire themselves out so that they could fall asleep upon returning to their bunks.

Several minutes of absolute quiet went by. Finally the voice said, "I have added a towel and two bottles of water and some other items to your gear to get you through the forest. Follow Arie's advice and don't look back. The forest is a dark and forbidding place. It is full of Craxies and other mean creatures wishing to do you harm. If you look back you will be tempted to return to the safety of BEBE. But you girls deserve your freedom! You must leave now. Goodbye and good luck. I shall miss both of you and that manic doll Sochi."

The pillow case was held up by whoever was behind the column. Jasmine took it without saying a word. Clearly, whoever it was meant them well. Moreover this mysterious, unidentified, person was very smart: she figured out the code in a few minutes and was able to read Arie's coded message.

It certainly could not be Sister Fa. But then who was it? The person clearly did not want to be identified. Jasmine was dying to find out who this helpful stranger was. But now was not the time to look a gift horse in the mouth.

Reader: The expression— *don't look a gift horse in the mouth*—refers to the time when people bought, sold, and traded horses. A lot could be learned about the horse by looking into its mouth, kind of the way people judge cars by looking under the hood. However if you got your horse as a gift it would have been rude to inspect the horse. I mean, for example, that if you get a shirt for a present you don't ask the giver if the shirt is made of the finest material.

Breathing a collective sigh of relief, the three of them made their way to the East Tower. Were their troubles over at last? Cortina began to walk towards the elevator but Jasmine pulled her back. "We are not returning to our room Cortina," whispered Jasmine. "We are escaping from BEBE remember? According to Arie's directions we need to walk down two flights of stairs to the exit door. The exit door will have a misleading sign on it that we'll ignore. Then we'll open the combination lock and be free."

They silently walked down the two flights of stairs leading to the exit. Sure enough they found a large, ugly, steel door with a sign that said:

Warning; keep away
This room contains the dangerous machinery that makes the calf's foot jelly.
If you don't want to end up as calf's foot jelly, don't open this door!

The sign was very frightening. Cortina began to shiver and started to go back but Jasmine held her by the hand. "I can't do this." Cortina said. "Suppose that Arie was wrong and this room really does contain the machinery to make the calf's foot jelly. Then we'll be ground up and mixed with the other ingredients that are used to make the calf's foot jelly and the BEBE girls will eat us!"

Cortina's warning frightened Jasmine. She put her ear near the door and listened. Yes, there was the noise of heavy machinery behind the door! Was Arie wrong?

Meanwhile Sochi had recovered from the experience of the encounter with the mysterious stranger. "What difference does it make if we get ground up or not," she said. "We're not here anyway!"

"Please button up your lip," warned an exasperated Jasmine who had started to sweat heavily even though in this part of BEBE it was unusually cool. "I don't want to hear another word out of you! I have to think!"

Jasmine was losing her cool. But Cortina was so close to panicking that if she guessed that Jasmine was close to panicking herself she would give up on the escape and run back to her room. It was absolutely essential for Jasmine to give the appearance of being calm. What was it that the mysterious stranger had said? *...Follow Arie's advice...Follow Arie's advice....Follow Arie's advice.*

That did it! It was now or never. Jasmine grabbed the strip of paper with the combination number 09-66-06 and tried to open the combination lock. It didn't work! She tried again. It didn't work! She tried a third time. Once again it didn't work! Jasmine had become desperate; her hand was shaking so strongly she had to sit down and rest. The strip of paper fell out of her hand and drifted to the floor. It came up as 90-99-60. There was just enough light from the blue floor light for Jasmine to make out the numbers. *What the heck*, she thought, *there was nothing to lose!* She tried 90-99-60 and

CLICK

the door opened!

A blast of cool forest breeze greeted the girls. Both girls raised their arms in victory and then embraced. They had done it! Even Sochi celebrated. "I've done it! I've done it!" she cried.

The machinery noise that Jasmine had heard and was meant to frighten them into returning came from a little speaker connected to a tape recorder. Sochi tried to destroy it but Jasmine held her back. "It doesn't belong to us," she said. "And besides, it failed to frighten us into going back."

Hand-in-hand the three of them walked happily down the path and began their journey into the forest that—they hoped—would eventually lead them back home.

25. Jasmine in the forest

Jasmine checked her watch and saw that it was nearly three o'clock in the morning. They had been walking fast and Jasmine figured that they had put at least three miles between themselves and BEBE. Other than the strange night forest noises one would normally hear in the forest at three o'clock in the morning there was nothing unusual to report. Sochi was fast asleep in the pillow case. Cortina suggested that they take a break and drink some of the water that their unknown friend back at BEBE had given them.

When Jasmine reached into the pillow case to retrieve a water bottle she was surprised to find a tickle stick there. "Look Cortina," she said with some amazement, "it looks like our mysterious friend gave us a tickle stick. I wonder what for?"

"Throw it away," said Cortina in disgust. "I hate those things. Once I saw Sister Do use it on a French girl that wouldn't eat her calf's foot jelly and the girl laughed uncontrollably for at least five minutes. It wasn't a pretty sight, let me tell you. We all felt sorry for Rire—that was the girl's name—and later we consoled her as best as we could. When I saw what these tickle sticks can do I decided that when I grow up I will spend my life fighting against tickle sticks. Perhaps I'll even join MATS: Mothers Against Tickle Sticks. Of course I'll have to be a mother first!"

To Jasmine this made good sense. The elimination of weapons of forced mass laughter (WFML) would make for a better world and she would join also. Perhaps she could convince Dorvit and Pilata to join MATS as well.

The forest quiet was suddenly pierced by a high-pitched screeching noise. Two small slithery, fluttering, creatures landed on Cortina's arm and gripped her skin. Cortina screamed and tried to shake them off—to no avail. Not knowing what else to do, Jasmine grabbed the tickle stick and touched one of the creatures. It immediately lost its grip on Cortina's arm, fell to the ground and went into convulsions. The other one flew off.

"What in the world is that?" asked a shaken Cortina. With great care Jasmine picked it up with her BiteNoMore™ gloves, which she had had the good sense to take along. She looked at the convulsing thing with her flashlight; it was horrible. It had large ears and a dog's snout and a pair of needle-like fangs for piercing skin. She had seen something very similar at the museum of natural history. It was the feared *Desmondus rotundus*: the tropical vampire bat! It fed on blood!

"Ugh!" cried Jasmine as she examined the creature. She threw it away and went to calm Cortina. "I think it was a vampire bat," said Jasmine." These scary things are usually found in tropical jungles. Maybe someone kept them as pets and when they required too much blood for feeding their owners released them into the wild.

After a while, Cortina and Jasmine calmed down. They drank some of the bottled water in silence. *The tickle stick had saved them,* thought Jasmine. *Their unknown benefactor had provided a weapon with which to defend themselves. Maybe she, Jasmine, wouldn't be so quick to join MATS after all.*

About ten minutes later Jasmine asked Cortina if she was ready to continue. Cortina nodded *yes* and put her bottle away. The girls smiled at each other. "Thanks for saving me," Cortina said. "I don't know what I would have done without you!"

"Without me you'd be sleeping comfortably in your bunk instead of walking through this dark and mysterious forest and being bitten by vampire bats," said Jasmine somewhat guiltily. "But maybe it'll all be worth it if we make it home."

"Yes but without you I'd be eating potato sandwiches and calf's foot jelly and collecting spider's silk all day long in that smelly room. I wouldn't get to see my family or friends. I'd have to do everything that the Monitors asked of me like an illegal immigrant servant. No matter what happens from here on I'm glad that I'm out of BEBE and that I'm here with you. I know you'll find a way to get us home."

The adventure with the vampire bats helped forge a strong bond of trust between the girls. *Its funny* thought Jasmine, *that in tough situations I seem to know what to do without thinking. Are there any professions that require this kind of skill?* But Jasmine couldn't think of any. All the professions she knew about required different skills; like knowing how to dress properly if you are the President of the United States; or knowing how to use a credit card if you want to be a successful housewife; or knowing how to make ugly faces if you are the leader of Iran or North Korea; or smiling a lot and saying "there's nothing to worry about," if you handle other people's money; or getting married often if you are a movie star; or sending out bills for large amounts of money if you work in a hospital; or knowing how to curse properly if you are a professional athlete.

Wait a minute, though Jasmine, *if I trained lions and tigers in the circus and they wouldn't listen to me or grabbed hold of my arm or leg, now that would be a tough situation and I would have to figure out what to do!* At that moment Jasmine knew what she wanted to be: a big cat trainer! That would make proper use of the skills that she had.

Suddenly Jasmine decided to check on Sochi. When she put her ear close to the pillowcase in which Sochi was being carried she could hear some murmuring. "There are only two choices," murmured Sochi to herself. "Either we are <u>here</u> or we are <u>not here</u>. But Jasmine brilliantly demonstrated

—using logic—that we are <u>not here</u>. Therefore we must be somewhere's else. But where then are we? Why won't Jasmine tell me?"

Jasmine smiled. "Poor Sochi, she is all confused. I'll explain it to her later."

Despite the fact that they had been walking for several hours it was still pitch black in the forest. By now Jasmine figured that they had walked some six miles from the BEBE castle. There was no chance that anyone from BEBE could catch them now. The only Monitors that would know that they were gone were Sister Fa and their unknown benefactor and neither one of them— for different t reasons—would tell Big Sister.

Up ahead, maybe a half a mile or so, they could see a light. "Do you think we have arrived at Magicland already?" asked Cortina, her eyes bright with hope. "No chance," said Jasmine. "Arie said that the trip through the forest might take as long as ten hours and then we would have to cross a stream. At most we've been walking for about four hours, probably a little less." The attack of the vampire bats consumed some time but Jasmine was not sure how much.

As they got closer to the light they could see that it was coming from a large bonfire. Large moving shadows fell on the thick grove of trees separating the girls from the meadow where the bonfire burned. They could hear screeching, cackling, yelling, and other rude noises. Jasmine signaled to Cortina to make herself less visible by crouching on the ground.

"What do you think is going on?" asked a tense Cortina. Jasmine didn't know but she was frightened. She and Cortina edged forward; what they saw made them freeze with fear.

Before them, in the forest clearing, about thirty creatures covered by white sheets were dancing around a large fire surrounding a huge stone carving— maybe ten feet high— of an enlarged macaca monkey. On the base of it it said: KING MACACA . Its designer was somebody named George Allen. Jasmine didn't recognize the name but she figured that anyone who could make such a big thing out of a small monkey must be very clever.

Reader: Members of the macaca monkey family typically have long tails and prominent cheek pouches. The family includes the macaque and rhesus monkeys and the Barbary ape.

The white-sheeted creatures were singing:

Oh mighty and dear King Macaca...
Mumbo-Jumbo, Sticky-Gumbo
Boomlay boom!

We gather in this forest dell
To beg of you to cast a spell
On naughty children far and wide
Whose faces we shall paint with pride

We think some children find it queer
When we the Craxies do come near
With cans of paint and brushes too
To paint them red and maybe blue

And as we dance and as we shake
These kids have made a big mistake
We'll cover them with sticky goo
Nancy, Frank and maybe **you**!

King Macaca

Then suddenly they stopped, removed their sheets, fell to their knees and began to pray to the great stone macaca. Yes they were the Craxies all right: rabbit heads and the webbed feet of frogs!

"What does it mean?" whispered a frightened Cortina. Jasmine, who had been studying this horrible scene very carefully, wasn't sure. "Maybe they are asking this macaca statue to cast a spell on kids so that they'll disobey their parents and go out in the middle of the night. Then the Craxies will make them miserable by painting them all over." *Could a stone statue actually cast a spell?* Jasmine had seen movies in which the ancient Egyptians prayed to stone gods and other people prayed to a golden calf. Didn't the parents of some of her classmates pray to a statue with the head of an elephants and the body of a human?

So maybe there was something to this business of praying to stone and metal statues. Otherwise why would people do it?

"Look," whispered Jasmine, "they haven't seen us. Let's retreat into the darkness slowly without making any noise. Then when we are out of earshot we'll quickly get away from here and continue going southeast to Magicland. The main thing is not to attract their attention by creating any kind of a disturbance!"

Worshipping the golden calf

Just then a loud JASMINE! could be heard coming out of the pillow case. It was Sochi! "Jasmine," she said triumphantly, "I figured out where we are since we are not here!"

Jasmine's hair stood up on end and sweat got into her eyes. "Shut up Sochi," she hissed. "It's a matter of life or death!"

Sochi did not have a strong voice. But her outburst had caught the attention of the Craxies who had keen hearing. They looked into the darkness where Jasmine and Cortina were crouching. In desperation, Jasmine picked up a rock and threw it in the other direction. The Craxies all looked to where the rock had fallen. "It's only a scared rabbit running through the underbrush." croaked a large, blue-headed, metal-studded Craxie in a voice that sounded like metal rubbing against metal, "Maybe we should dip him in orange-colored paint. Then the foxes and wolves will have no troubles finding him! Ha-ha!" Blue-head seemed to be the leader.

Jasmine thought that this would have been a very cruel thing to do. Now she not only feared the Craxies; she hated them too. They were much worse than Waxface who basically had a gentle soul. They also were much worse than the Tilops who, while greedy and foolish, were not cruel. For the first time she thought about teaching the Craxies a lessons that they wouldn't soon forget.

Even before Jasmine and Cortina had a chance to creep away, the Craxies got up, arranged themselves into a single file, put their sheets back on, and began to leave the forest clearing. They didn't walk but rather leapt in small steps, the way frogs tend to do, all the while screeching in a single grating voice:

> Boomlay, boomlay, boomlay, boom!
> Boomlay, boomlay, boomlay, boom!
> Find the kids by light of moon!
> Give us paint and a solid broom!
> We'll make of them a flower bloom!
> Boomlay, boomlay, boomlay, boom!
> Boomlay, boomlay, boomlay, boom!

Reader: The lines *Boomlay, boomlay, boomlay, boom,* are part of a poem— *The Congo*— written by one Vachel Lindsay. In a part of New York City called Flushing some parents and children greet each other on Fridays, by common agreement, by saying *Boomlay, boomlay, boomlay, boom!*

Jasmine and Cortina viewed this scene with a mixture of awe, relief, and contempt. To relieve the aches and pains from crouching for so long the girls stood up and dusted themselves off. It felt good to move arms and legs again. After standing there for about ten minutes, Cortina urged Jasmine to continue walking. "The Craxies must be far away by now. Isn't it safe for us to leave?" asked Cortina. But Jasmine was deep in thought and didn't answer right away. Finally she turned to Cortina and with a resourceful smile said, "Look Cortina, I have a plan. By pure chance we came across the Craxie forest headquarters. I think that no other human in the world knows about this place except for us. The Craxies, of course, don't know that we know about this place. They probably believe that they get their power from that statue of ugly King Macaca. Maybe now is a chance to teach them a lesson that they won't soon forget! But I won't do anything unless you first agree."

Cortina didn't know what to think. On the one hand she wanted to leave this awful place and get on with their trek to Magicland and ultimately back to their homes. On the other hand her dislike and fear of the Craxies was almost as strong as that of Jasmine. By golly maybe now was the time to do the right thing! "Let's do it!" she said to Jasmine. "Just tell me what you want me to do!"

"OK," said Jasmine. "The first thing is to find where they keep their paint and brushes. Then we'll paint King Macaca a whole bunch of different colors and make him look as silly as possible. But we'll leave room on the base of the statue to write a message to the Craxies. The message will tell them to stop gluing and painting children. The Craxies don't seem all that smart; they'll think that the message comes from King Macaca. Maybe that will convince them to stop hurting kids."

> **Reader:** The base of a statue is sometimes called a *plinth*. Do not use this word unless it is absolutely necessary. Repeated utterances of the word *plinth* may lead to serious tongue problems that will require professional attention.

Cortina was delighted by Jasmine's idea and grateful that she could help. She didn't realize it yet but under Jasmine's influence she was turning from a meek little girl, whose life was being controlled by others, into a mini-warrior.

The girls left their hiding place in the forest and carefully approached the meadow where the Craxies had gathered. The bonfire had gone out when the Craxies had thrown sand on it before leaving. The girls approached King Macaca with some fear; perhaps the statue really did have magical powers.

They looked at the statue to see if they could detect any movement. But the statue didn't move: they figured that it probably was just a brainless carved rock. To make sure Jasmine threw a stone at it but nothing happened. Then Jasmine spoke to it and said *You big stupid monkey* and still nothing happened. Then Cortina followed Jasmine and called it *You ugly scary thing* and still nothing happened.

Finally, to make absolutely sure that King Macaca was just a silly piece of carved rock, Jasmine pulled Sochi out of the pillowcase and asked her to say something mean to King Macaca. This was the kind of thing that Sochi loved to do. So she tried to kick the plinth and called King Macaca *a sorry excuse for a statue and if she, Sochi, were a dog, King Macaca would be her favorite fire hydrant; she would use him day and night.* Both girls were taken aback by Sochi's outburst; if that wasn't going to get a rise out of King Macaca then he truly was just a silly piece of carved rock. But, again, nothing happened.

The girls began to look for where the Craxies kept their paint and brushes. Cortina found a wooden cover just behind King Macaca. When she lifted the cover she found a wide, shallow hole containing several cans of Sherwin-Williams paint and Home-Depot glue and an assortment of brushes. She gave the thumbs-up sign to Jasmine and the girls went to work.

Jasmine painted King Macaca's head blue and his arms orange. Cortina painted his body purple with white stripes on his bottom. Sochi painted a moustache on his face and a black eye patch over one of his eyes. Then Jasmine had another idea: she painted white tears coming out of King Macaca's other eye.

When they were finished it was time to write a warning to the Craxies. The girls debated what to write; Sochi suggested *I am not here so where am I?* But that was rejected by both Jasmine and Cortina. After a few minutes of brainstorming the girls came up with:

> Macaca, monkey king of kings
> That's me. I've done some awful things
> The sight of me will make you sad
> Because my deeds have been so bad
> Craxies! Stop your evil ways
> Or short will be your wretched days!

The girls were very happy with this message and quickly wrote it in white paint on the plinth. Then they turned all the paint cans over and buried the still-wet brushes in sand. Their work was finished; if only they could stay to watch the faces of the Craxies when they returned! But that wasn't possible.

The girls had done a great service to the children of the world.

It was time to go.

> **Reader:** If you like what Jasmine and Cortina wrote you might want to look up the poem *Ozymandias* by Percy Bysshe Shelley.

26. Jasmine and Cortina meet the unicorn

Except for a brief break during which they drank some water and ate some of their apple pie, Jasmine and Cortina had walked steadily for nearly three hours. On the eastern horizon they could see the first reddish lights of the rising sun. The glimmer of light lifted their spirits and they began to chatter about what they would do when they got back home. "You know," said Cortina, "we are like two little birds that begin to chirp when the first rays of sun appear." Jasmine laughed and said, "Let's not get too happy yet, we still have a long way to go. We may not have to worry about the Craxies anymore but who knows what other dangerous creatures are in the forest."

At the very instant that Jasmine finished her sentence, both girls heard quarreling voices not a hundred feet away. They immediately fell to the ground and listened.

"For the twentieth time I told you not to call me Corny! Would you like a little poke from my horn the next time you forget to call me by my real name?" said a strong voice with a horsy twang.

"I don't say Corny just to tease you; I call you Corny much to please you!" came the answer. The second voice sounded like the braying of a donkey.

"Well you are not pleasing me at all. No sir! Not at all!" was the horsy reply.

"But Corny is your common name! For that your daughters share the blame!" said the donkey voice.

"My daughters! May they each suffer from rotten teeth; from large warts; from pinched hooves! They are not my daughters anymore!" said the horse voice.

Following this outburst Jasmine and Cortina heard loud, pitiful weeping and the donkey voice saying "There, there, no need to cry. Troubles come and troubles fly."

For their part the girls didn't think that these creatures—whatever they were— represented a serious threat. Nevertheless Jasmine reached into her pillow case and withdrew the tickle stick. Just in case!

Suddenly the donkey voice said, "Behind those trees two girls lie low. Shall we go and say hello?"

The girls barely had time to get up before they faced a sad-looking unicorn and a much smaller donkey. The unicorn looked like a large white horse with a three-foot long golden horn sticking out of his forehead.

"Stay back," warned Jasmine. "I hold in my hand the terrible tickle stick. One false move and you'll both be convulsing with laughter on the ground!"

"Please dear girls, we mean no harm. We come to celebrate your charm!" said the donkey softly.

The unicorn looked carefully at the girls. "My heavens," he said. "What are these creatures? Of what possible use are they?"

"My dear Corny," said the donkey, "they are humans and they don't bite. We need not hurry to take flight. They are born tightly curled and have no use in our world."

"Well, I beg to differ with you," said an annoyed Jasmine. "We have lots of uses. We help our parents finish off the food they buy! We take piano and violin lessons! We go to ballet classes! We go with our mothers to buy new clothes! We play with our dolls! We..."

But she was interrupted by the donkey who said, "Enough my dear. Do not protest! What we said, we said in jest."

"Well that was a silly joke," said Jasmine, "but I forgive you. My name is Jasmine and this is my friend Cortina. A few hours ago we escaped from a place called BEBE and now we are trying to get to Magicland where we expect to get help to get home."

"My name is Sneer, King Sneer, to be exact. My attendants and courtiers call me "Sire' as I expect you to do. This hapless donkey here, who plays the fool, is supposed to amuse me. His name is Foolscap. But he doesn't amuse me at all. No sir! Not at all!"

"My dear girls," Foolscap whispered, "Be patient with my nervous master. Else he'll anger even faster."

King Sneer looked at the girls with admiration. "You girls actually escaped from BEBE, the black castle? You must have extraordinary courage! But you were very lucky. Very lucky indeed! Between here and the black castle is the headquarters of the Craxies. Had you run into the Craxies you would have ... You would have..." Suddenly King Sneer began to cry. Clearly the king was depressed about something.

"But the girls are here, and safe they are. From the Craxies, they are far." said Foolscap in an attempt to console the king. "You see girls," said Foolscap in a low voice, "The king is very sentimental; especially since he's become environ-mental." As he said that, Foolscap raised his front right leg and used it to make a circular motion near his temple: the standard 'hand' signal to indicate that someone is crazy.

"Look Sire," said Jasmine addressing the king. "There is no need to walk around with a long face. As it happens we did see the Craxies but they didn't see us. Cortina and I left a message for them that said that they must change their ways. Maybe they will."

Jasmine felt sorry for King Sneer. Tears were still rolling down his cheeks. She went over to him and patted his flank. Cortina did the same. "There is no need to feel sad, Sire" said Cortina. "You are a fine-looking unicorn and your friend Mr. Foolscap clearly loves you. So what's to be sad about?"

"You've opened, girls, a can of worms! You must now hear what Corny yearns!" whispered Foolscap. "The king's story is long and sad. But listen, please, or he'll go mad."

King Sneer composed himself. Pretty soon the tears were gone and he began to speak. "First of all I'm NOT a unicorn. There is NO such thing as a unicorn except in silly stories and fables that you read to kids when they can't sleep! I am a tri-horn, that's right, a tri-horn! Tri-horns are rare but they do exist! A tri-horn has three straight horns. The herds that I ruled were all tri-horns. They all had two regular horns and a third horn that was smaller but still easily seen.

King Sneer continued. "Ordinary horses and cows envied us of course. The tri-horns were a symbol of our noble lineage from Hornmesses the second, the great tri-horn ruler of the 19th dynasty of ancient Egypt.

In my clan we were very fortunate; all of us had three large straight horns. But I was particularly fortunate: my horns were made of gold!"

"How did that happen?" asked Cortina.

"As you may have learned in your biology class, most living things have metals in their bodies: a grain of gold, a bit of silver, a touch of copper, a pinch of iron, a dusting of zinc. For reasons that only that smart Mr. Darwin can explain, I accumulated a tremendous amount of gold in my body and it all migrated to my horns. That's why I have golden horns!"

Reader: Mr. Charles Darwin was a great scientist whose *theory of evolution* can explain why animals look the way they do. But remember: Mr. Darwin's theory is only a theory!

"But Sire, you have only one horn," said Jasmine. "Not three!"

"What you just said was not so smart!" whispered Foolscap. "You may have broken the king's heart!"

The king began to sob. Many tears fell from his long face. Jasmine and Cortina patted him gently and calmed him with soothing words. "There, there," they said. "Good Sire, good Sire." Neither Jasmine nor Cortina had any experience in giving comfort to a sad tri-horn king. But their experience in soothing unhappy dogs and cats helped them to deal with the king's sadness.

"Let the king tell his story," announced Foolscap, "else we'll all be sorry!"

King Sneer finally stopped sobbing. "Because I had these gold horns, the herd decided that I should be king. I was a good king: tough but fair. In time I married and raised three daughters. The eldest was Gangrena, the middle one was Radona, and the youngest was Cordillera. The entire herd, including my daughters and I grazed happily above the cliffs of Dover."

"They grazed atop the cliffs of Dover since there they found a lot of clover," added Foolscap.

"Is Dover near Lalaville?" asked a puzzled Jasmine. She wasn't sure where this conversation was going.

"Dover's on the English shore. Right above the ocean's roar," said Foolscap.

King Sneer looked at Foolscap with annoyance. "You think you could be quiet for a few minutes so I can tell my story to these brave girls?" he said.

"Sire, go on and please continue. I did not know you had in you." said a subdued Foolscap.

Jasmine was getting annoyed with the way that Foolscap talked. She wished that he could talk like a normal donkey.

"So one day, while grazing, I felt a crick in my knee and a crook in my neck. Or maybe it was a crook in my knee and a crick in my neck, I don't remember. The pain made me realize that I was getting old," said the king, "and it was time to give away my gold horns to my children.

"The king's good health was wearing thin. Gangrena could not hide her grin!" whispered Foolscap. Jasmine ignored him. "Please let the king tell his story," she said with some heat.

The king continued with his story. "To test whether they deserved my gold horns, I called a meeting of my daughters and I. I asked each one how much they loved me. Gangrena said that she loved me more than life itself. So I gave her a gold horn and made her rich for life. Then Radona said that she loved me more than the sun, and the moon, and all the stars put together. So I gave her my second horn and made her rich for life."

"What happened to Cordillera?" asked Cortina.

"Aha! Here lies a tale of scorn from last of daughters born." said Foolscap.

King Sneer's eyes moistened. He was near to crying but Jasmine said, "Please Sire, we all want to hear the rest of the story, especially what happened to Cordillera."

The king controlled himself. "When I asked Cordillera how much she loved me," he said, "she answered that she loved me the way a daughter loves a father, not more not less. What kind of an answer is that? Moreover, she said that if she got married and had children she would love her husband and her children as much as she loves me now. Can you believe that? Is that a way for a daughter to speak to her father? What ingratitude! Of course I didn't give her my third horn and I told her to leave the field of clover in Dover."

Jasmine was confused. To her it seemed that Cordillera gave a very reasonable answer. In fact, to Jasmine, Cordillera's answer made more sense than those of Gangrena or Radona. She thought that the king was being selfish. If he expected Gangrena to love him more than life itself how could she ever love her children or husband? But maybe now was not the time to question the king's judgment.

"So what happened after that?" asked Cortina who was getting a little impatient. On the one hand she wanted to hear King Sneer's story. On the other hand she wanted to get on with their trek to Magicland.

"With the golden horns I gave them, Gangrena and Radona became very popular with the young tri-horn stallions. Until then they weren't so popular because Gangrena had smelly feet and Radona suffered from excess gas. Soon they married. Gangrena married a simpleton who didn't realize what a bad person she was; his name was Balveny. Radona married a brute whose name was Stonewall. After I gave them the golden horns they had no further use for me. Pretty soon—during a terrible storm— they kicked me out of the clover fields of Dover. Boy was I miserable!"

"Ingratitude these daughters showed. And seeds of hate in Corny sowed." whispered Foolscap to no one in particular.

"Sh!" hissed Jasmine and Cortina at the same time. "Let the king go on with his story!"

"That's right! I'm still the king! Every inch a king!" cried King Sneer.

"Yes Sire, you are, Sire," said Jasmine. "Please continue."

King Sneer continued his narrative. "Cordillera, bless her heart, eventually married a French general by the name of Francois Poltron, also known among his soldiers as Francois *Le Faible*. When she found out how badly Gangrena and Radona treated me, she convinced Poltron to attack her sisters and their husbands. Her plan was to kick out Gangrena, Radona, Balveny, and Stonewall from the clover fields of Dover and send them all packing to Death Valley in California.

"Wow," said Cortina, "Death Valley!" That doesn't sound like a nice place!"

"That's a place of heat and sand, where the sturdy come unmanned!" said Foolscap in a tone of awe.

"That's right!" said King Sneer. "It wasn't supposed to be a nice place! But that fool Poltron brought along rubber arrows instead of real ones and water pistols instead of real guns and lost the war to Balveny and Stonewall. Stonewall put Cordillera in prison and treated her terribly. That's where she is at this very moment."

"That's awful!" said Cortina who was on the verge of crying. "Is there anything we can do to help?"

"They want so much to help, from a love that's deeply felt. For my king they seek relief; so strong and noble is their belief," thought Foolscap. Foolscap was very moved by Cortina's offer of help. But what could two young girls armed only with a tickle stick do?

27. The trip to Spoon River

"I can't tell you how much good it does this royal Sire to have two intelligent girls like yourselves listen to his troubles. I don't suppose we could arrange for me to visit with you on a weekly basis? I could pay you to listen to me and my medical insurance would pay me back." said the king. "Right now the only creature that I can talk to is my faithful Foolscap here. But since he's a mere donkey, I'm not even sure that he understands the anguish that has seized my heart!"

"A donkey is not a flunky, Sire. A donkey may be no gazelle but a donkey, Sire, can listen well!" said Foolscap whose feelings were obviously hurt. "My ears are long, my nose is droopy, but as of yet I'm no one's groupie."

King Sneer gave Foolscap an affectionate look. Then he turned towards the girls and said, "I owe you a favor for the kindness that you have shown me. Is there anything that I can do to repay you?"

Jasmine and Cortina exchanged glances. Finally Jasmine said, "Dear Sire, it is with regret that we must turn down your kind offer to pay us to listen to your troubles. We want to get home and see our parents again. That is why we are struggling to get to Magicland across from Spoon River. There a magician by the name of Max will help us find the way home. Also Sire, my friend Cortina and I are not licensed to offer you advice in a professional capacity. But I give you my word that if we can figure out a way to free Cordillera you will be the first to know."

Foolscap turned towards the king and said, "These girls are wise, despite their size. They will free good Cordillera, perhaps with help from Yogi Berra."

Jasmine had never heard of Yogi Berra. She would look him up on Google™ when she got home. "That's right Sire," said Jasmine. "Remember it ain't over till it's over."

Reader: Yogi Berra was a famous philosopher who spent many years in the Bronx, New York. In his spare time he played baseball for the New York Yankees.

"Then let me give you a lift to Spoon River," said the king, much encouraged by his discussions with the girls. "It will save you a lot of time and it will delay the time when we must say goodbye."

"Never reject a ride that's free," said Foolscap. "Therein lies my philosophee."

It wasn't so easy for the girls to get on the back of King Sneer. First they had to climb up to reach the back of Foolscap. They did this by Cortina standing on Jasmine's shoulder and lifting herself onto the donkey's back. Then Cortina helped Jasmine get onto the donkey by letting Jasmine grab her hand and pulling herself onto his back. Once both girls were safely seated on Foolscap's back they rested.

Jasmine, Sochi, and Cortina on the back of King Sneer with Foolscap looking on

"Why can't we ride on Foolscap's back?" whispered Cortina to Jasmine. "It will be much easier than having to climb up on the king's back."

But Foolscap heard Cortina's question. "When the king gives you a lift, 'tis *his* back that is the gift!" cautioned Foolscap in a voice so low that King Sneer didn't hear a word.

So once again Cortina stood on Jasmine's shoulders—while Jasmine sat on Foolscap back— and reached up to grab the king's back. Then Jasmine pulled herself up using Cortina's arm as a lift. Eventually both girls found themselves securely seated on the king's back. They were both exhausted from their efforts and sweat was running into their eyes. Hopefully all this effort would enable them to make up for lost time.

"Do you know the way to Spoon River?" asked Jasmine after she managed to catch her breath. "Arrive we shall at the River Spoon well before the hour of noon," answered Foolscap. "Sire knows this darkened land like the back of his own hand."

"But the king doesn't have any hands. He has four legs and four feet." exclaimed Jasmine.

"The landscape's known in Sire's head. It's time to go, enough's been said!" answered an irritated Foolscap. Clearly he didn't like to be corrected.

"Hold on tight," said the king. Once I get started, I gallop like the wind!"

"He gallops like the wind—or so they say. Better move aside to give him way!" whispered Foolscap to no one in particular.

It was true though; the king galloped just like a horse. In fact if he didn't have the large golden horn and the two golden horn stubbles he could have easily been mistaken for a large white horse. As much as he tried, Foolscap had trouble keeping up. It was only when the king stopped for a drink at a pond or stream, or to nibble at some grass that Foolscap caught up with them.

The little girls clung to each other in great fear of falling off the king's back. They passed streams and trails and boulders and mushrooms and pine trees. They saw rabbits and coyotes and various creepy things. They heard and saw white owls and red and yellow crickets and red-winged blackbirds. They had to duck to avoid hitting their heads on low-hanging branches of maple and oak trees. They rode up hills and down into valleys. They passed fields of blue and purple flowers and various prairie grasses. They listened to the distant howls of wolves and the trumpeting of geese. But mostly they heard the whine of the wind as it flowed past their ears and felt the wind's abrasive power on their cheeks. But this didn't bother them for they knew that with every stride they were getting closer to Spoon River and Magicland just beyond it. By now BEBE and the Monitors and the vampire bats were far behind them. Even the Craxies were not a threat anymore, or so they thought.

Had they forgotten that the forest held creatures that meant to do them harm?

28. Two surprise encounters

As the group approached a little clearing the king stopped and said, "We are quite close to the Spoon River. Another half hour or so of galloping and we'll be there. Perhaps you girls want to refresh yourselves; you know, drink some water and eat some of that apple pie I saw in your sack."

If truth be told, the girls were more than happy to stop. For one thing their bottoms hurt from all the riding at such a furious pace. For another, they felt cramps in their legs from sitting on the king's back. An exhausted Foolscap fell to his knees and muttered, "From all this haste I need a rest; the king does run with too much zest."

It was much easier getting off the king than getting on. Cortina simply moved one leg to the same side as the other leg, twisted around while holding on to the king's back, and let herself fall to the soft earth. Jasmine watched her carefully and did the same thing. Because Jasmine was a little heavier than Cortina, she fell with a louder thud but she wasn't hurt. Both girls were happy to get some circulation back into their legs; they were also thirsty and hungry.

"Sochi has been quiet for the longest time," said Jasmine to Cortina. "I wonder what she's been up to." Jasmine felt a little guilty about ignoring Sochi for so long; she had been thinking about the king's problem especially how to free Cordillera.

Reader: That's how it is in the real world as opposed to fairy tales: we ignore our next of kin in favor of dreaming about fabulous adventures!

Jasmine looked into the pillow case and found Sochi writing on a piece of paper. "What are you doing Sochi?" asked Jasmine in a friendly way. "I am writing my memoirs," answered Sochi without looking up. "I am keeping track of all that's happening. People all over the world will remember what I wrote during our escape from BEBE."

Jasmine was intrigued. "Can I have a look at what you've written?" she asked. With some reluctance, Sochi let her see the paper. "Remember I'm not finished yet! This is just the beginning of a 12,000-word manuscript." What Jasmine read shocked her to the core. Moreover there was something vaguely familiar about it.

Sochi's memoirs

Four score and seven hours ago my Jasmine brought forth to this crazy place a new idea, conceived in ignorance and bravado, and dedicated to the proposition that a good adventure beats all.

Now we are engaged in a fight for survival against vampire bats and Craxies. History is testing whether that idea, or similar stupid ideas, so rashly conceived and so dedicated to narcissitic impulses, can long endure. We are met in a clearing in a dark forest. We have been reduced to drinking water and eating crumbs of pie. Perhaps a portion of this clearing will become our final resting place. If it does become our final resting place, it is altogether fitting and proper that Jasmine should go to rest first!

The world will sharply note, and long remember what I've written. The world will never forget the great things that I did here. It is for me—Sochi—to dedicate myself here to the unfinished work that I have so nobly advanced. I will give my last measure of devotion so that I, Cortina, and Jasmine shall not perish from the earth.

"What kind of nonsense is this?" hissed Jasmine. "The things that happened to us were not my fault! And even if some of them were, I don't see where you come off claiming 'all the great things that I did here'! Exactly what great things did you do? And what is this stuff about me 'going to rest first'?"

Sochi did not expect such a bitter response. She crossed her little arms and pursed her lips and at first said nothing. Then, just before retreating into the pillow case, she said, "I am not going to pursue this conversation any further. You are clearly out of control!"

"I'm out of control am I?" cried Jasmine. "I'll show you how out of control I am!" And with that Jasmine went to grab Sochi but it was too late—Sochi has sought shelter in the back of the pillow case, behind all the stuff that the two girls had put in there. For Jasmine to get to Sochi she would have had to remove the entire pillow case, something she was not prepared to do.

Cortina, who was watching all of this with a big smile on her face, burst out laughing. When Jasmine saw Cortina laugh, she burst out laughing too. What was the point of getting angry at Sochi? Sochi was a doll—not more nor less—and what can you expect from a doll? A doll had a doll's brain and a doll's sensibilities and you had to accept her for who she was. The fact was that Jasmine loved Sochi very much and if you love someone you have to make some room for their nonsense.

After eating the remains of their pie and drinking some water, Jasmine and Cortina rested with their backs against a large oak tree. The king was quietly munching on some grass and Fooslscap was dozing off. It was a quiet, peaceful, scene—the kind you see in 17th century Dutch paintings in museums.

Reader: If you want to get a taste of what the scene was like look into the grove of trees in the center of the painting *Wheat Fields* by Jacob van Ruisdael in 1670.

Jasmine couldn't help but notice how sharp the king's horn was. "With a horn like that," she thought, "you could easily protect yourself against wolves, bears, even tigers and lions."

Suddenly Foolscap jumped up and screamed in pain. "By ugly vampires I've been bitten. My poor, poor self has been smitten!" he yelled. Sure enough two slithery, fluttering, vampire bats had landed on his rear and inserted their sharp little teeth in his bottom. Foolscap's braying was so loud that Cortina had to put her fingers in her ears to keep out the noise.

To Jasmine it was déjâ-vu all over again. She recognized the vampire bats as being the same ones that had attacked Cortina shortly after they entered the forest. Without a second thought she reached for the tickle stick in her pillow case and ran to Foolscap who was obviously in pain. With a quick flic of her wrist she touched the bats, first the one then the other. Both released their grip on Foolscap and fell to the ground. The sight of the two bats with their blood-smeared mouths convulsing on the ground was too much for Jasmine and Cortina; they had to turn away.

"My dear friends," said the king in a somber voice. "Please turn your back on this scene. I must do something that I don't want nice little girls like you to witness."

Jasmine and Cortina followed the king's instructions. Behind them was heard the sound of motion and struggle followed by a loud 'Oof!' and soon followed by another loud 'Oof'!' Then they heard the swishing sounds of two objects being hurled through the air. Finally they heard the sound of two objects landing maybe two hundred feet away among the dark trees.

It's OK to turn around now," said the king

When the girls turned around the bats were gone. In their place was some disturbed earth and scattered leaves. Clearly there had been some sort of struggle. The whole experience had left the girls shaky.

"What shall we do when they come back?" asked Cortina. The king looked at Jasmine and Foolscap and then turned to Cortina. "They won't be back, my dear. You need not worry. But now it's time to continue our trek. We are near the end."

Said Foolscap, "Sire, these girls are tired. If they don't rest we'll soon be mired. Let them ride upon my back. Power and strenght I do not lack." The king nodded *Yes*; Cortina and Jasmine were very grateful to Foolscap for his suggestion. The thought of all the work required to get onto the king's back, especially in their present distraught state, was too much.

They left the clearing without talking: King Sneer at the head and Jasmine and Cortina on Foolscap's back. They walked slowly; the mood was solemn, no doubt induced by the struggle with the vampire bats. Jasmine hated violence but, she thought, sometimes violence is required to rid the world of evil. She had a good idea of what happened to the bats. She preferred not to think about it.

By now the sun had cleared the horizon but the high canopy of the forest trees admitted little light. Suddenly it got brighter. "Look," said an excited Cortina, "look at all the points of light in front of us!" Jasmine looked; what she saw made her happy to the core. It was the glint of the sunlight reflecting from the river. "Is that the Spoon River?" she asked excitedly.

Foolscap's eyes watered over; pretty soon some tears began to flow. In a sad voice he said," 'Tis the river where friendships part; for us the end, for you a start." They walked a few more paces and came nearly to the river's edge. The king had a mournful expression on his face; he looked like he was about to cry also. Jasmine and Cortina were seized by a great sadness—they were about to leave two good friends behind. In a flash Jasmine had a terrible thought: Is this what life was all about? Leaving friends everywhere and anywhere? She had left her parents; she had left Dorvit and Pilata (hopefully she would see them and her parents again); she had left her good friends at BEBE; she had left her unknown benefactor who gave her water and the tickle stick; and now she was going to leave two wonderful friends who had cared for her and protected her. Gosh, what a bummer!

Suddenly Jasmine came out of her reverie and realized that everything around her had gone quiet. The king stood motionless with a grim expression on his long face. Foolscap stood absolutely still with his ears erect and his lips pulled back over his teeth. Cortina, who sat in front of Jasmine and blocked her view, had gone white as a sheet and sat motionless on Foolscap's back. For a moment Jasmine thought that they had all turned into wax. Did she turn into wax also? No, she could move her arm and turn her head. As she twisted her head around Cortina's body so that she could see what was happening up front, she saw the single most terrifying sight of her whole life: on either side of the king stood some fifteen Craxies with brush in one hand and a can of paint in the other. Right in front stood their blue-headed, metal studded, leader.

"What do you want with us?" asked King Sneer. "I warn you that my horn is sharp and my trusted servant Foolscap is skilled in the art of combat."

"Yyeess, I,...,I have great might; I won't give up without a fight!" stuttered Foolscap. He looked like he was about to faint.

"Leave us alone," screamed Sochi from inside the pillow case, "or you'll feel the wrath of my mistress Jasmine, you miserable monkey worshipper!" "Shut-up," hissed Jasmine to Sochi; fortunately Sochi's voice through the pillow case was so weak that blue-head didn't hear her. In fact had blue-head heard what Sochi said, especially the 'monkey worshipper' part, our story would have had a tragic ending.

For what seemed like a long time nothing was said. Finally blue-head came close to the group and spoke. "My name is Kimono Sabbatarian but you can call me Kimosabee. We come in peace. Our ruler King Macaca, Lord of the lakes and forests, Spirit of the growing things, Astral Father of the Earth before people were people, fish were fish, and horned things were, er, horned things, has been angered by our evil ways. He has destroyed our stocks of paint, buried our brushes, and left us a message that warned us that 'short will be our days if we don't mend our evil ways' or words to that effect."

Kimosabee looked around to see if his words had made an impact. Satisfied that everyone was listening with rapt attention, he continued:

"We the Craxies have met and discussed King Macaca's warnings. By a vote of 21 to 9 with one abstention we have decided to devote our lives to helping the poor, right the wrong, hunt down the criminals, expose the tax cheats, and provide quarters for motorists who need to feed the parking meters. Do not be afraid of our paint and brushes. We have come here to bury our brushes not to raise them. We shall empty our lead-free, non-polluting, non-toxic, US-made, paint into the Spoon River."

"We want to do something decent with our lives," wailed Kimosabee. "Help us to impress our great ruler King Macaca that we are a force for good and not for evil."

Silence, mixed with great relief, greeted the end of Kimosabee's speech. Then Jasmine had a brilliant idea.

"Kimosabee your Excellency," said Jasmine, "I have a wonderful suggestion for how you can demonstrate to King Macaca that you are a powerful force for good. But first let me introduce myself: my name is Jasmine and this is my friend Cortina and we are on our way to Magicland."

"Yes, I am Cortina and after Sochi, I am Jasmine's best friend." said Cortina.

"And I am King Sneer, every inch a king, and this is my trusted servant Foolscap," said the king.

"Yes I'm smart and aim to please though I'm no Maimonides," said Foolscap, giggling at his own joke and fluttering his eyelashes.

> **Reader:** Moses Maimonides was a great Jewish/Spanish philosopher and doctor who was known for his smarts. He lived during 1135-1204.

After the introductions were made, all the Craxies politely hopped from one leg to the other five times. This was their way of approving the manners of the four strangers they had just encountered.

"But dear lady," said Kimosabee, "please let us hear your wonderful suggestion for how we can demonstrate to King Macaca that we are a force for good."

"Well it's like this," said Jasmine, "The king needs some help in getting his loyal daughter Cordillera out of prison, where she is being held by his disloyal daughters Gangrena and Radona and their husbands. But it is better that the king tell his story by himself."

"'Tis better the story the king provide; to get these Craxies on our side." whispered Foolscap to King Sneer.

So the king told his story in great detail to the Craxies. Some of them openly wept when they heard of how he got kicked out of the fields of clover in Dover during a terrible storm. Others began to do cartwheels and yoga stretches—signs of great distress in the Craxie culture—when they heard of what the vicious Stonewall and foolish Balveny had done to the king.

"...And so my friends, I ask you to help me liberate Cordillera and send my disloyal daughters and their criminal husbands to Death Valley." concluded the king in his address to the Craxies.

"It's there that they will have the time... to think about their monstrous crime," added Foolscap sternly.

After the Craxies calmed down from hearing the king's story, they went into a huddle to discuss what was to be done. After several minutes, Kimosabee emerged from the huddle and addressed the king. "King Sneer, let it be known to all that we pledge our unwavering allegiance to you and will help you get Cordillera back. However justice must be tempered by mercy. To send these miscreants to Death Valley where they will have no access to food and water is a violation of the Universal Laws of Justice. Instead we propose to send them to Long Island, New York. There they will have to dodge criminal children, deal with crooked auto mechanics, get stuck in backed-up highways, breathe smog and diesel fumes, endure endless shopping centers, pay enormous taxes, and—best of all—run-up mortgage bills that will send them to the cleaners! As for you kind king, we have the means to send you and your trusted servant back to the fields of clover in Dover. One of our group is an investor in the Conrad-American steamship line and he will arrange to provide excellent, first-class accommodations back to Dover for the two of you!"

King Sneer and Foolscap reflected on what Kimosabee said. "Such punishment for each of four! You could not want to ask for more." advised Foolscap to the king. "Moreover when we get to Dover our long ordeal will then be over."

Jasmine and Cortina hoped that the king would agree to what the Craxies offered. They waited a few tense moments. Finally the king raised his head, looked around, and smiled. "It shall be as you say," he said in a loud voice. "The hour has come when creatures of reason, such as ourselves, show the mercy that has been implanted in us by the great Creator of all things. In a short time Cordillera will be free and the others will be sniveling in Long Island, New York. Today I am proud to be an Englishman!"

The girls looked at each other; they had no idea that King Sneer was English. Moreover he didn't look like a man; by his own admission he was a tri-horn with two horns missing. Maybe that's what made him an Englishman. Jasmine suddenly realized that there were many things that she didn't know. She resolved to pay more attention to what Miss Acapela taught in school. The look on Cortina's face revealed that she was having similar thoughts.

A great cry of joy went up from the Craxies, the king, Foolscap and the girls. After they dismounted from Foolscap, the girls hugged Foolscap and the king, and gave the thumbs–up to the Craxies (there was no way that they going to hug the Craxies—they were, like, so ugly).

As the girls approached the river's edge, they heard Foolscap say:

"By this river we now part,
There is no joy in this one art,
We wish you luck in what's to be,
May the Lord watch over thee."

The girls' faces were wet with tears. Pretty soon their feet, then their ankles, and finally their legs were also wet but this time from the Spoon River's cold waters. The stream ran swiftly but remained shallow. Jasmine had no trouble holding the pillow case over her head; the only danger was to fall from slipping on one of the slippery rocks at the bottom of the stream. Fish brushed their legs as they crossed the water. When they got near to the other bank the girls turned around to give one last wave goodbye.

But King Sneer, Foolscap, and the Craxies were gone. Only the deep forest and the dark-green trees could be seen. There were no other signs of life.

As they reached the other side and mounted the river bank they saw a large sign surrounded by blinking colored lights.

"Welcome to Magicland," it said.

29. Magicland

The girls wanted to look their best in this new world they were about to enter. So they went back to the river, washed their faces and combed their hair, rinsed out their socks, and adjusted their clothes. If you had looked at them you would never have guessed that in the last twelve hours they had gone through life-threatening travails. Their unknown benefactor from BEBE had left a towel in the pillow case that the girls used to dry themselves with. Other than the fact that they were hungry, they looked fresh and healthy.

The gardens of Magicland

By now the sun was up, and the darkness of the forest had given way to an open, colorful landscape. Before them lay the most spectacular scenery that they had ever seen: beautiful landscaped gardens; decorative stone bridges and lanterns; carefully tendered lawns and ornamental mazes; baobab trees and sculptured bonsai; and fields of red and yellow flowers.

"It is a beautiful place but does anyone live here?" asked an astonished Cortina. It was not a question that Cortina expected Jasmine to answer because Jasmine wouldn't have known any more about this place than she. The place reminded Jasmine a little of a tiny park in the very middle of Lalaville that—while not as beautiful as this place—had some of the same elements: some ornamental bushes, stone lanterns, beds of flowers and so forth. But in Lalaville, there were signs to remind you that you were in that other, coarser, world, for instance:

Danger: Lyme disease ticks are present.
Warning: No loitering after 11:00 pm.
No alcohol allowed in the park.
No dogs allowed.
No littering and spitting.
No ball playing.
No skateboarding.

No eating or drinking.
No yelling, singing, or noise-making.
No playing of radio.
No cursing or using vile language.
No indecent gestures.
No signs of excessive affection.

But here in Magicland there were no such signs, in fact nothing to remind you that the other world even existed!

The girls walked on a pleasant red-brick path leading to a little stone bridge. On the other side of the stone bridge they could see an oval lawn surrounded by elegant wooden benches. The place looked inviting and the wooden benches would be a great place to take a rest and maybe even a nap.

When they got to the lawn and made ready to take a nap, they were startled to hear a voice addressing them. "This is private property and no one is allowed here except private people," said the voice. They looked around but saw no one. Suddenly, emerging from behind a large banyan tree on the edge of the lawn was a tall black man dressed in a tuxedo and top hat, with a rabbit-eared bandicoot on his shoulder.

Jasmine readied the tickle stick. "I don't know what you mean by private people," she said in a firm voice, "but my friend Cortina and I are *people* and we like our *privacy*. Does that make us private people?"

"It certainly does!" said the tall black man in a now much-friendlier voice. "My name is Boredock Abomah but my friends call me Max and I am a magician by trade," said Max. "And whom do I have the pleasure of addressing?"

Upon hearing that they had finally met Max the magician, Jasmine felt much relief. "My name is Jasmine and this is my friend Cortina," said Jasmine. "We are very, very, very happy to meet you. We have been told that you will help us and my doll Sochi get back home to our parents.

Max reflected on what he had just heard. "How do I know that you are who you say you are?" he said. "My magical powers are limited and I save them only for the people who really need me. Can you prove that you really are the Jasmine and Cortina that escaped from BEBE? That you are the Jasmine that reformed Waxface and tricked the Tilops? That you are the Jasmine who helped convert the Craxies from a vicious gang of graffitists to a force for good?"

For a moment Jasmine experienced a shock of panic. Without her camera-phone, video camera, digital camera and MP-3™ recorder how was she expected to prove that she had done all these things. But then she remembered that Arie had given her a four-line poem that would establish her identity with Max; she hoped that she could remember the poem. Suddenly it came back to her! Standing straight before Max she said:

> *Oy Vay, Oy vay, I have to say*
> *Help us, Max, to find our way*
> *If we get lost, I must confess*
> *We do not have a GPS!*

It worked! Max nodded his head in approval and said, "You are indeed who you say you are! I will help you but the task of getting you home will not be easy. It may take a few days. In the meanwhile I will try to make things as comfortable for you here in Magicland as possible. But first are you hungry?"

"Yes!" both girls cried at once. Max smiled and whispered something to the bandicoot on his shoulder. The bandicoot jumped to the ground and disappeared behind the banyan tree. Within seconds it came back with a bag of warm cinnamon rolls and two containers of orange juice. The girls fell on the rolls and the juice the way two tiger cubs would fall on their first meal after not having eaten for a week. Nothing was said while the girls ate; the only sound came from the munching noises that the girls made while wolfing down the food.

"You know," whispered Cortina to Jasmine, "this Magicland is pretty good. If it wasn't for wanting to see my family and friends so bad, I might want to stay here."

Jasmine was shocked at what she heard. But the truth was that Magicland seemed even better than Sao Rico or Locoloco. She had to agree with what Cortina said.

30. First day in Magicland

After the girls finished their cinnamon rolls, Max told them that he was occupied with learning some new, complicated, magic involving turning men's ties into little snakes. He advised the girls to explore Magicland on their own and to meet him back at the oval lawn at 6:00 pm. If they had to take a nap, he said, it was completely safe to do so. It never rained in Magicland and it never got too hot or too cold.

Sochi, meanwhile, had woken up from a long nap and climbed out of the pillow case to examine her new surroundings. As soon as she saw the bandicoot—whose name was Banjo—she took a dislike to him. Straining to make her voice as loud and threatening as possible, she cried, "Don't start making like you're some kind of royal creature just because you're standing on someone's shoulder. To me you're just an overgrown mouse with a wormlike tail and ugly rabbit ears."

Sochi's words did not sit well with Banjo. But being shy by nature, he couldn't think of an appropriate response except to say, "Sorry, I didn't quite hear what you said." Banjo's answer gave Sochi the lead she was looking for. "You talkin' to me? I dooo believe that you talkin' to me! Better watch what you say or I'll make you swallow your tail!"

Jasmine told Sochi to stop talking in this rude and insulting manner. "I'll put you back in the pillow case if you don't behave," she said. "What's come over you anyway? Do you think that you are a taxi driver?"

At the moment Sochi had no wish to go back inside the pillow case. So she shut her mouth and proceeded to ignore Banjo; but it had been a mistake to insult him. Banjo had a calculating mind and was already planning his revenge.

"Why do you think that they call this place Magicland," asked Cortina of Jasmine as they walked near a pond covered with water lilies. "I haven't seen any magical stuff here— have you?" Just as Jasmine was getting ready to reply that she hadn't either, a cluster of large soap bubbles floated by, each with a yellow and black butterfly in it. "Wow!" cried Jasmine. "How in the world did Max get the butterflies inside those soap bubbles?" It was one of the most astonishing sights the girls had ever seen. They now began to understand that this place was like no other place that they had ever been to.

Just as they began to recover from what they had just seen, they heard some splashing sounds coming from the pond. What they saw now was even more amazing than the butterflies in the soap bubbles: a whole bunch of goldfish doing synchronized water aquatics and all jumping out of the water at the same time while holding little green umbrellas as parachutes. And if that wasn't strange enough, right in front of them a black-and-white colobus was painting a bench with his long bushy tail, all the while smoking a pipe.

Butterflies in soap bubbles and jumping goldfish

This was all too much for the girls. They sat down on a bench overcome with wonder at the bizarre events taking place around them. No sooner had they sat down than a blue ring-necked parakeet— with a coleopteron on its back to help navigate—landed on the bench and said that dinner would be served at the oval lawn at 6:00 pm. In its beak the parakeet held a menu, which he dropped in Jasmine's lap. The menu said:

Black tie Diner at 6:00 in the Evening
(Ladies and Gentlemen Will be Dressed in Formal Attire)

Children's Menu

Premier (first course)
Chocolate Milk au Froid

Seconde (second course)
Les Viandes (meats)

Hot Dogs with Mustard in Buns

Les Legumes (vegetables)
Corn on the Cob with Melted Butter

Troisieme (desert)

Chocolate Cake with Vanilla Ice Cream

"Wow!" said Jasmine to Cortina. "It looks like we'll get yummy hot dogs and corn-on-the cob in butter and chocolate cake with ice cream for dinner. But we'll have to put on nice dresses. Where in the world are we going to get nice dresses? All I've got are these jeans, a tee-shirt, and this sweater. From the looks of things you don't have much more either; and how about Sochi? She looks like a rag doll! "

"I do not look like a rag doll!" screamed Sochi from inside the pillow case, where she had gone to take a nap. "All I need is for someone to comb my hair and repack my stuffing. Even you, Jasmine, are capable of doing that!"

It was all too much for the girls. They fell into a deep sleep and dreamt of white clouds, songbirds, fields of flowers, and their families.

31. Max does his magic

At five thirty in the afternoon, the blue ring-necked parakeet appeared and woke the girls with loud screams of Skreet!... Skreett!... and left a note for them to come to the oval lawn. The girls woke, yawned, stretched, and tried to remember where they were.

"I don't know if I dreamt this or not," said Jasmine, "but I seem to recall that we are supposed to have a fancy dinner at six this evening with Max and his bandicoot, Banjo."

"It was no dream," said Cortina. "But we have a problem. Max expects us to come well-dressed to this dinner; and all we have are t-shirts and jeans. Do you have any ideas?"

Jasmine didn't have any ideas. Still she didn't want to annoy Max by refusing his invitation so she urged Cortina to go back with her to the oval lawn and explain to Max their circumstances. When they got back to the oval lawn, they were greeted by Banjo who held three plastic shopping bags. "In these bags," he said, "you will find the appropriate clothes for the dinner. If you look on the left—behind the tree—you will see a little house made of bamboo. Inside the house are dressing rooms where you can change. Max is still working on his magic trick; he will join us in a little while."

Sure enough the girls found attractive clothes in the bags. There was even a fancy little dress for Sochi. Each of the girls received a blue silk dress, tights, black patent leather shoes, and a diamond-studded gold hairpin for fastening the hair. A similar ensemble, but in miniature, was there for Sochi. Sochi, of course, was initially delighted; little did she know that Banjo gave her an outfit that didn't fit right. Banjo was taking revenge for the rude way that Sochi had spoken to him.

After the girls dressed they admired themselves in the wall-length mirror in the bamboo house. Each helped the other with adjusting the clothes properly and placing the hairpin in just the right place on the head. If truth be told the girls were somewhat inexperienced with dressing in fancy clothes. This was the time that they wished that their mothers were around to help them. Still, everything fit just right; even the shoes were a perfect fit.

For Sochi it was a different story. When Jasmine tried to dress her all she got from Sochi were cries that the dress was too tight; that the hairpin scratched her head; and that the shoes were squeezing her feet. "Nonsense," said Jasmine. "Max and Banjo knew our sizes exactly. Why wouldn't they know yours?"

Sochi didn't know why. But the fact was that she could barely breathe in her dress and in order to get her feet inside the shoes she had to bend her toes. When they left the bamboo house and Sochi saw the bandicoot with a smirking smile on his face she suspected a dirty trick. But what could she do? She had no evidence that Banjo was responsible for her discomfort and she didn't want to be told that she was paranoid if she complained to Jasmine.

In a little while Max appeared; he looked happy and excited. "Girls," he said, I've mastered a remarkably difficult trick that no one in the world except the magician Almazut was able to do. Almazut was the magician in the court of King Zitava in twelfth century Bohemia. Unfortunately he lost his memory in a tragic accident before he had a chance to explain how he did the trick. The accident resulted when Almazut put a tea kettle on his head and asked one of the palace guards to hit it as hard as he could with his mace. Almazut was sure that by saying the magic words *Hak mir nisht ken tshaynik* he could stop the mace from crushing the tea kettle and hurting him. It didn't work. The blow caused Almazut to develop permanent amnesia. He ended up working for King Zitava as a tax collector."

Both girls quivered from the vicarious pain they felt upon hearing this terrible story. Still they waited with anticipation for Max to do his trick.

Max took out six ties from his pocket. He asked the girls to handle the ties and verify that these were ordinary ties; Sochi insisted that she handle the ties also. The girls and Sochi agreed that there was nothing unusual about the ties: they were made in Mexico from a mixture of polyester and silk. They were actually very beautiful: one showed a large ketchup bottle and smaller bottles in the background; another showed a bunch of dogs playing cards; a third showed a bunch of flying, laughing, piglets; a fourth showed colorful beetles; a fifth showed cows eating grass; and the last one showed a colorful assortment of hot peppers.

Jasmine was so taken by these ties that she almost wished that she was a boy so that on special occasions like weddings and funerals and important holidays she could get to wear them.

Max stood quietly and put the ties in his fist. Then he closed his eyes and appeared to sleep standing up. Finally he yelled *Ooplah*! and threw the ties on the ground. But when the ties hit the ground they turned into six cute little blue snakes that very quickly crawled into the grass. It was an amazing sight! The girls had never seen anything like it!

Jasmine was now convinced that Max could do anything; even get her back to Lalaville. She beamed with pleasure and hugged Cortina.

 Meanwhile the bandicoot had prepared a lovely table full of delicious food. The girls had expected to see at most four regular chairs—one each for Jasmine, Cortina, Max, and Banjo—and a high-chair for Sochi. Instead they saw seven chairs and Sochi's high-chair. Jasmine wondered who the other guests were.

When they were all seated at the table, Max stood up and holding up a glass of oyster juice said, "I have invited some of the most learned men in Magicland to have dinner with us. Please welcome Doctors *Zwei*stein, *Drei*stein, and *Vier*stein; Doctor *Ein*stein, having given his brain to science, asked to be excused."

As if on cue, three stooped, elderly, men with long gray beards and all dressed in black appeared at the edge of the lawn; in no time at all, they had seated themselves at the table and began to drink the oyster juice.

Jasmine noted that the elderly men all wore gold pins in their lapels that said 'Genius'.

The dinner was outstanding for everyone — for everyone that is—except Sochi. She was served a tiny plate of high-bran cereal (good for emptying the colon) and a tiny glass of sour cranberry juice (good for the kidneys and bladder). When she looked up from her plate, in disappointment, she saw that Banjo was smirking at her. Overcome by rage she picked up her glass of cranberry juice and got ready to throw it. But Jasmine, ever mindful that everything should go right at this point in their adventures, gave her a look that said *if you do that you will spend the rest of your life at the bottom of the closet in solitary confinement*! Sochi got the message: she hunched her little shoulders, crossed her arms, and looked down at the table with her mouth turned down at the edges.

Max was addressing the learned men. "You see gentlemen, the Magicland blimp is ready to take these two girls back to their homes but we have a problem. As you know the blimp will deliver them in their yards at home in the middle of the night. At that time of night everyone is asleep and no one will notice what is going on."

The three learned men stroked their beards and nodded their heads in agreement.

"But," said Max, "how will the girls explain to their parents that they have been gone from home, without permission, for nearly a whole week? There is a very real danger that their worried parents will be sufficiently angry so that they will send the girls to BEBE for correctional behavior. I don't think that these poor girls deserve that do you?"

This problem had not occurred to Jasmine and Cortina. Suddenly their good spirits plunged: the thought of going back to BEBE was a real bummer! Sochi looked like she was going to cry.

"So you see," said Max addressing the three Steins, "I am counting on you to solve this difficult problem."

The three learned men conferred. Jasmine listened carefully but caught only snatches of their conversation *"...e equals emcee squared... speed of light... inertial coordinates... frame of reference... space-time fabric...metric tensors... worm holes...black holes...no holes...time slows down...velocity tensor.. .mazel und bruches..."*

The conference over, Doctor *Vier*stein was delegated to explain the solution. "Ahem," he began, "Our colleague Doctor *Ein*stein came up with a *theory of relativity* that will help us. Naturally this theory was developed before he gave his brain to science. In Doctor *Ein*stein's theory, time is not a constant but slows down when you go very fast. So if you are going very fast in, say, a spaceship one hour of time on earth may be only one minute in the spaceship. The theory says that all you have to do is put the girls in the Magicland blimp, crank up the engine and circle the planet Earth 2,844,305 times at a speed of 185,389 miles per second. This will cause a week to pass on earth but only seconds to pass in the girl's experience. The week of unaccounted-for time will be erased by this action."

Doctor *Vier*stein looked around to see if everyone was following. The bandicoot was wolfing down his fourth hot dog, Sochi had fallen asleep, but Max and the girls were listening carefully. He then resumed his explanation.

"When the girls will see their parents, the parents will not be aware that the girls were gone for nearly a week. The parents will believe that the girls spent a restful night in their beds and got up in the morning, as usual, to have breakfast."

While the girls didn't understand the details of the theory, they and everyone else cheered Doctor *Vier*stein's explanation. "You know," said Jasmine to Cortina, "that business with time being relative is pretty obvious. Think about it: When you're at the movies seeing a good film, an hour seems like a minute. But when you're stuck in school on a nice sunny day, a minute seems like an hour."

Cortina agreed. "I know that when I go to the dentist a minute feels like an hour but when I'm playing with my friends two hours seem like a minute!"

The girls looked at each other and smiled. Both had the same idea at the same time: *Great minds think alike!*

"I have to tell Max to have the Magicland blimp drop me off at 8 Schuyler Road in Lalaville," said Jasmine. Suddenly she had a terrible thought: she and Cortina were going to be separated perhaps never to see each other again! Oh no!

"Wow!" said Cortina. "I live at 130 Wildwood Street, also in Lalaville. It is right around the corner from you! This means that we can see each other all the time and be best friends!"

When Jasmine heard what Cortina said she felt a joy like none she that ever felt before. Not having had a sister, Cortina was the closest thing to a sister that she would ever have. Jasmine felt like she was hearing violins playing beautiful music and walking through a gentle rain of rose petals. It was one of the happiest moments of her life.

But a sour note came from Sochi who had wakened and caught part of the conversation between Jasmine and Cortina about time being a relative quantity. "You mean to say that this Doctor Einstein became famous for saying that in the dentist's chair a minute seems like an hour but when you're playing with your friends an hour seems like a minute? What rubbish! Why would anyone bother to listen to such an obvious fact?"

Dinner was almost over. Max rose to make a little speech, "I wish to thank Doctors *Zwei*stein, *Drei*stein, and *Vier*stein for providing the solution to the difficult problem of getting these girls back to their homes without parental reprisals. I also want to thank the girls for their excellent behavior while guests in Magicland. It is now time to consider how lucky we are to be living in..."

Banjo quickly jumped on Max's shoulder and whispered something in his ear. Max turned slightly red and seemed embarrassed. He continued with: "My aide-de-camp Banjo reminds me that now is not the time for long speeches. We must prepare the girls for their voyage home. To that end they will go back to the bamboo house and exchange their dresses for space suits. There is a small spacesuit for Miss Sochi, which will keep her stuffing safe during the rapid acceleration from zero to 185,389 miles per second. Before take-off the girls will be shown a movie so boring that they will fall asleep and not wake up until they have safely been returned to their homes."

"What's the name of the movie?" asked Cortina. "It is a movie by the Swedish director Indebar Boreman. It is called *The Triumph of Friggy the Frog*," answered Banjo. "Believe me it's even more boring than *Fanny, the Flea that Wouldn't Fly*.

Neither of the girls had seen *Fanny, the Flea that Wouldn't Fly* but they had seen *The Triumph of Friggy the Frog* at BEBE and boy—was it boring!

Within an hour the girls had changed from their pretty blue dresses into spacesuits and were sitting in the cabin of the Magicland blimp. Extra fuel was required for the 2,844,305 times around the Earth. The crew consisted of a pilot, co-pilot and two flight attendants. Just before the movie started the flight attendants announced that this was a non-smoking flight and that seat belts needed to be solidly fastened. Over the loudspeaker came the message: "When we reach our cruising altitude of 400 miles and our cruising speed of 185,389 miles per second, the flight attendants will come around to serve soft drinks and snacks. Now sit back and relax and enjoy the movie."

At the point in the movie where Friggy asked his teacher "Dear Mr. Axelrod: What's the difference between ignorance and apathy?" the girls dozed off. They couldn't hear the colossal roar of the engines nor see the blinding white-hot exhaust coming from the back of the blimp. They couldn't feel the tremendous acceleration that enabled the blimp to go from zero to 185,389 miles per second in just three minutes. They couldn't see the planet Earth spinning beneath them faster than the wheels of a car going at sixty miles per hour.

When the blimp reached its cruising speed of 185,389 miles per second it became extremely quiet. Except for a weak light in the cabin, all was dark. The blackness and enormity of outer space passed the girls by; they and Sochi were in the deepest sleep of their lives.

32. Space travel

On a small asteroid in our solar system, only a few miles in diameter, one of its 1532 inhabitants was scanning the skies with a homemade telescope. As he aimed his telescope at the planet Earth and saw the blimp spinning around its periphery at ultra-high speed he turned towards his mate and said, "Someone is sure in a big hurry!"

33. Home at last

The Magicland blimp landed in Jasmine's yard at four o'clock in the morning. A sleepy Jasmine was asked by the flight attendants to exchange her space suit for her tee-shirt and jeans. She was given her pillow case, which contained Sochi, and personal items. Sochi could be heard snoring and muttering, "That's right; we are somewhere's else and that somewhere's else is Panama and I can prove it."

Cortina had already been dropped off around the corner at 130 Wildwood Street. She was completely asleep and the flight attendants had to make themselves invisible in order to bring her into her bedroom to put her in her bed.

Since Jasmine was awake, but barely so, the flight attendants didn't have to carry her. Instead they led her to the back door that exits to the yard and opened the door using a Never Lockout™ device that Max had purchased from the Scylla and Charybdis Company for three easy payments of $19.95 plus shipping and handling. When they made sure that Jasmine had made it to her bed, they removed the tickle stick from the pillow case, but left all the other items inside with Jasmine. Then they returned to the yard, locked the back door, and re-entered the Magicland blimp. Flight commander Rashi and his co-pilot Akiba started the small ion engine to get them into space. After that they would turn on the massive thermo-atomic engine, which would bring them back to Magicland in a few minutes. They could not afford to turn on the thermo-atomic engine in Lalaville: the roar of the engine and the blinding flash of its exhaust plume would have wakened and panicked the whole population of the village. The hot exhaust gases would have generated a temperature of a hundred million degrees!

Other than that the night passed uneventfully.

Ж   Ж   Ж

"It's a good thing that today is Saturday and she doesn't have any school," said Chacha to Caesar. "I've never known her to sleep so late and here it is, almost ten o'clock in the morning and she is still asleep. Also I wonder if she forgot to brush her teeth last night; I didn't see the usual bits of excess toothpaste she leaves behind in the sink. I hope she's OK!"

"What are you worried about?" said Caesar. "She was fine last night although she was a little upset that Dorvit regarded her only as her second best friend. Dorvit had told her that Pilata was her first best friend."

"I wish that Jasmine wouldn't depend so much on Dorvit and Pilata. They are nice girls but Jasmine deserves someone more loyal." said Chacha. "Maybe she'll meet some nice girls in camp this summer."

Upstairs, Jasmine gave the first stirrings of waking up. She looked around and took in the familiar surroundings. "Sochi! Wake up!" she said. "I've had the wildest dream anyone ever had!" But Sochi was hard to wake; she kept muttering, "Yessir Madam, we are not here. We are somewhere's else and that somewhere's else is Rangoon!"

Sochi's words sounded very familiar to Jasmine. Did Sochi have the same dream? And how come she, Jasmine went to bed last night in her jeans and tee-shirt? Did she forget to put on her pajamas? And what was that funny pillow case doing on the bedcover?

Jasmine went to the pillow case and found two empty plastic water bottles, a strip of paper, and two envelopes, one pink and one blue.

The strip of paper said:

Dear Jasmine:

This is the last note from your friend Arie. I hope that you made it home OK. There are many rumors at BEBE: that you've been kidnapped by the Craxies; that you have decided to stay in Magicland; even that you have been adopted by King Sneer. But I know better; you are the type of little girl that stays the course. And in your case the course was to get home to your parents and friends. I miss you a lot and if you were a spider I would ask you to join me in making webs.

There are two things that I want you to remember: 1. Honor your mother and father; and 2. if you see a spider don't kill it—it might be related to me. I have thousands of cousins all over the world. They are hard-working and law-abiding.

Many hugs and little non-poisonous bites (instead of kisses, which spiders can't give).

Love
Arie

When Jasmine read the note, tears came to her eyes. So the whole adventure was no dream! It actually really happened! Good old Arie; how she missed him! If it had not been for him she would still be a prisoner at BEBE.

Next she opened the opened the blue envelope. It said:

Dear Jasmine:

I want to tell you how much we enjoyed your stay in Magicland. Banjo misses you almost as much as I (but he's glad that Sochi is gone) and the three Doctor Steins have asked if you got home safely. I wish that you hadn't been in such a hurry to leave. Had you stayed a little longer you could have gone to our yearly bandicoot ball where banjo invites all his friends and they entertain us by doing bandicoot folk dances.

If you ever need anything please e-mail me at <u>Maxmagic@magicland.org</u> *. This e-mail address will work only for you. Do not share it with anyone else.*

Best of luck

Max

PS: Remember: magic is great but love is better.

Wonderful Max! He really came through for her! She felt that somehow, somewhere, she would run into him again.

Meanwhile Sochi had wakened. "Jasmine," she cried, "I had a dream like you wouldn't believe! But where are we? Are we here or somewhere's else?"

Jasmine smiled. "We're here silly. Now shush so that I can read this letter."

Jasmine opened the pink envelope. Inside was a note in beautiful handwriting. It said:

Dear Jasmine:

I was the one that you encountered just before you escaped from BEBE. I hope that the water bottles and tickle stick that I put into your pillow case helped you and Cortina in your long and dangerous journey back home.

Please try to think of the Monitors at BEBE in a positive light. To many people on the outside we are ugly and threatening. But remember that many of the girls at BEBE really do need lessons in better behavior. If it wasn't for us they might grow into teenagers and adults that cannot adjust to the demands of society. For most of the girls, their experience at BEBE has made them better people later in life. They even become fond of dwarfs (haha).

The Monitors at BEBE do not have children of their own. The girls at BEBE 'become' their children. There is a great deal of love at BEBE but it is of the "tough love" kind. I and some of the other sisters actually cried when you left. Your kindness to the spiders was not overlooked.

I will remember you with great pleasure for as long as I live.

Sister Mi, as in <u>mi</u>dget

Jasmine put the note down. It was the most moving thing she had ever read. She was overcome with a feeling of great sadness.

But her sadness rapidly gave way to joy: her mother had called from downstairs, "Jasmine come down and answer the phone. There is a girl by the name of Cortina that wants to talk to you."

The End

Made in the USA